T0196012

To save her cozy Florida diner, Gia Morelli must choke down a heaping helping of murder....

New York native Gia Morelli is just getting used to life in Florida when she gets word that the town government wants to shut down her pride and joy: the charming little diner known as the All-Day Breakfast Café. A forgotten zoning regulation means that the café was opened illegally, and hard-boiled council president Marcia Steers refuses to budge. Gia is considering hanging up her apron and going back to New York, but before she gives up on her dream, she discovers something shocking in the local swamp: Marcia Steers, dead in the water. There's a secret buried in the books at town hall, and someone killed to keep it hidden. To save her café and bring a killer to justice, Gia and her friends will have to figure out a killer's recipe for murder....

Also by Lena Gregory

The All-Day Breakfast Café Series
Scone Cold Killer
Murder Made to Order

MURDER MADE TO ORDER

An All-Day Breakfast Café Mystery

Lena Gregory

LYRICAL PRESS
Kensington Publishing Corp.
www.kensingtonbooks.com

Lyrical Press books are published by
Kensington Publishing Corp. 119 West 40th Street New York, NY 10018

All Kensington titles, imprints, and distributed lines are available at special quantity discounts for bulk purchases for sales promotion, premiums, fundraising, and educational or institutional use.

To the extent that the image or images on the cover of this book depict a person or persons, such person or persons are merely models, and are not intended to portray any character or characters featured in the book.

Special book excerpts or customized printings can also be created to fit specific needs. For details, write or phone the office of the Kensington Special Sales Manager:
Kensington Publishing Corp.
119 West 40th Street
New York, NY 10018
Attn. Special Sales Department. Phone: 1-800-221-2647.

Kensington and the K logo Reg. U.S. Pat. & TM Off.
LYRICAL PRESS Reg. U.S. Pat. & TM Off.
Lyrical Press and the L logo are trademarks of Kensington Publishing Corp.

First Electronic Edition: June 2018
eISBN-13: 978-1-5161-0463-5
eISBN-10: 1-5161-0463-3

First Print Edition: June 2018
ISBN-13: 978-1-5161-0466-6
ISBN-10: 1-5161-0466-8

Printed in the United States of America

Nicky, I love you so much, and I'm always so proud of you!

Chapter 1

"Fools!" Savannah Mills swiveled back and forth on a stool at the All-Day Breakfast Café counter and tapped a steady rhythm against the butcher-block countertop with her long, powder blue nails. "Every last one of them."

Gia Morelli scrubbed the already spotless counter one more time for good measure, then flung the dishcloth into a bin beneath the counter, the steady *rat-a-tat-tat* of Savannah's rhythmic drumming making it almost impossible to think straight. "What I don't get is how they think they can get away with this?"

Earl snorted. The elderly man, who'd been the All-Day Breakfast Café's first customer, and had since become a friend, had made a habit of arriving at the café before they opened and lingering over coffee until Gia officially unlocked the door and started cooking. "The council members are so used to doing whatever they want with no opposition they're like a pack of spoiled brats."

"Yeah, well, not this time." Gia checked the clock—just about time to open. She rounded the counter and headed for the door. "No way I'm giving up everything I've worked for because that bunch found some antiquated zoning mistake."

"How are you going to get around it, though?" Earl asked.

"I have no idea. Yet." Gia unlocked the door, then dragged the chalkboard with the day's specials out onto the sidewalk and set it up. She looked up and down Main Street. Winter in Boggy Creek was certainly milder than the harsh bite of winter in New York, and yet there was something inside her, a small niggle of homesickness, that missed the change of seasons. Still… If she was going to give everything up and go back to New York,

After settling them with coffee and their menus, Gia retreated to the kitchen. She grabbed tongs and moved a few slices of bacon and sausage from the warming trays to the grill, then started scrambling three eggs.

Maybelle Sanford. It figured. That woman was destined to be a thorn in her side. She'd only worked—to use the term loosely—at the café for a day, and yet she kept coming back to haunt her. Since Maybelle had accused Gia of murder last time she'd seen her, it was hard not to jump to the conclusion she had something to do with the zoning fiasco. And yet...

Gia had been ready to fire Maybelle for being so lazy. Useless as a steering wheel on a mule according to Savannah. That being the case, it was hard to believe Maybelle had found the ambition to search for a way to close the café.

Gia dismissed any thought of Maybelle. Nothing she could do about it right now anyway, and all it was doing was aggravating her. She'd have to wait until Tommy called Savannah back. If not for his wife having their first baby last month, he'd have been at the latest council meeting, and she might have had a heads-up. As it was, she'd have to wait for him to get caught up.

She drizzled a small amount of oil onto the grill, let it heat until it sizzled, then poured the eggs onto the hot oil. While they cooked, she spooned out a serving of grits and one of home fries, which Earl had added to his usual breakfast after the first time he'd tried hers. She filled a bowl with gravy, dropped two biscuits onto a small plate, and set the dish on the cutout counter between the kitchen and dining room.

Earl ate an unbelievable amount of food for breakfast every day while still managing to stay rail thin. The man was in remarkably good shape for almost eighty years old, despite consuming a week's work of fat each morning.

She'd miss this if she had to give up the café. She enjoyed cooking, and she'd enjoyed making friends in Boggy Creek. In addition to Earl, there was Trevor, who owned the ice cream parlor down the street, Savannah, who'd been a good friend for years, and Hunt, who she held out hope would become more than just a friend. She dismissed the thought. Detective Tall, Dark, and Gorgeous was the last thing she needed to concern herself with at the moment.

She'd even gotten used to the solitude of living in her small house at the edge of the Ocala National Forest. Sort of. Thor helped. It was hard to believe Savannah had to talk her into getting the big Bernese Mountain Dog puppy. Now, she had no clue what she'd do without him. He made her life complete.

"Here you go." Willow rushed in, ripped the top page off her order pad, and stuck it above the grill, then frowned. "Are you all right?"

"I'll be okay." She smiled. "As soon as I get past being blindsided and figure out what my options are."

"If I can do anything to help, just let me know."

"Thanks."

She grabbed Earl's breakfast order and headed back to the dining room. Willow was a good kid and a hard worker. She'd also become a friend.

Another plus in the stay-and-fight-for-her-café column.

She started the next order. Unfortunately, she hadn't had much luck finding a cook after Maybelle and her replacement both hadn't worked out—or in Maybelle's case, just hadn't worked—which left Gia stuck in the kitchen all day. As much as she loved cooking, she really wanted to get out from in front of the grill and get to know her customers a little better. If she was going to make this work, she might have to give in and hire a cook. Third time's the charm? She certainly hoped so.

Truth be told, Boggy Creek was growing on her. At least, the people were. The critters, not so much.

The sound of raised voices right outside the kitchen pulled her attention.

Gia set the finished order on the cutout for Willow, pulled off her apron, and draped it over a stool. She strode through the doorway but stopped short when she ran into Savannah and a woman she didn't know in the hallway outside her office door. "Everything okay?"

Savannah peeked into Gia's office, then glanced at the other woman and pulled the door shut. She tucked her hair behind her ear, a nervous habit Gia had become familiar with when they'd lived together in New York. "Gia, this is Marcia Steers."

She only recognized the name because she'd recently received the letter from the council with Marcia Steers's name scrawled across the bottom and her title, Council President, typed in bold print beneath it. Gia eyed the woman standing in front of her, then swallowed her anger and extended a hand. "It's nice to meet you, Ms. Steers."

A hot pink sundress clung to Marcia's ample curves, and bleach blond hair framed her round face in a mane of over-teased frizz. High-heeled, leopard print sandals laced up her calves. She sneered and folded her arms across her chest. "Ms. Morelli."

Okay. Gia lowered her hand. "What can I help you with?"

"I want to discuss something with you." She raked her gaze over Savannah. "In private."

Savannah offered her sweetest smile. "As I already told you, Ms. Morelli is working. She will be happy to meet with you after the café closes."

Marcia ignored her, instead homing in on Gia. "And as I already told Ms. Mills, I need to speak with you."

"Actually, I'd like to speak with you as well." She forced a smile. "I'm hoping we can clear up the zoning mistake so I can keep the café open."

"There's no mistake, Ms. Morelli." Though Marcia's expression remained hard, her gaze darted repeatedly between the closed back door to the parking lot and the swinging door to the dining room. She stood stiff, like a cornered animal. "The café will close. The matter I must discuss with you is of a more personal nature."

Savannah eyed Gia and gave a discreet head shake behind Marcia's back.

Great. Now she had to either irritate Marcia, the woman who quite possibly held Gia's fate in her hands, or go against Savannah, which she couldn't do. She cracked the swinging door to the dining room open and peeked in. Willow had already seated several more tables and was taking an order. "I'm so sorry, Ms. Steers, but I'm the only cook, and I can't leave the kitchen just now. Can we meet later on?"

Marcia eyed her for a moment, then relented. "Fine. I want to look into something anyway. The café is closed on Mondays, right?"

"Yes."

"I'll meet you here tomorrow around noon."

"Sounds good. I—"

Before Gia could finish speaking, Marcia shot Savannah a dirty look, whirled away from Gia, then shoved through the swinging doors into the dining room.

Gia stared after her. "Maybe I should have just talked to her."

Savannah blew out a breath. "And what about your customers? Are you going to make them sit and wait while you two have it out in the middle of the café?"

The fact that she was right did nothing to lessen Gia's apprehension.

"She's clearly agitated about something. A public confrontation is the last thing you need right now." Savannah shook her head, then opened the door and walked into Gia's office. "Besides, I was helping Willow out, pouring coffee while people waited to order their breakfast. When I looked up, I caught sight of someone heading through the doors toward the kitchen. I couldn't tell who it was, so I came back to see what was going on, and I found Marcia coming out of your office."

Savannah shuffled through a small stack of papers on the desk. "You should really go through these and see if anything's missing before you meet with her."

"I guess—"

"Gia?" Willow stuck her head in the doorway. "Is everything all right?" she asked for the third time since arriving.

Gia needed to get her act together. "Umm...yeah."

Willow frowned but let it drop. "I just put three orders up, and one of them is a group of seven."

"Got it." She quickly scanned the papers on the desk. There was nothing of importance that she could see, but she'd have to look more carefully later. "Thanks, Savannah."

"No problem. But I think I'll give my brother another call." She looked up and caught Gia's gaze. "And maybe you'd better think about calling a lawyer."

Chapter 2

Gia stepped over a large branch blocking the path through the woods, then patted her pocket—for the millionth time—to make sure her canister of bear spray was still there. Though she enjoyed their walks, which allowed her to spend time with Thor and provided both of them some much needed exercise, her nerves sometimes got the better of her. This morning was no exception.

Thor trotted happily alongside her, sometimes darting ahead, but always staying on the trail and within sight.

She didn't have the heart to call him back, even though she wasn't in the best mood this morning and her mind was a million miles away. Unfortunately, her hectic schedule at the café didn't allow much time for hiking, or anything else for that matter. So she trudged on, despite wanting to go home and spend her morning curled up with a good book.

Savannah and Trevor had both insisted early morning hikes would clear her head and help her get used to living at the edge of the forest. Though they did help her focus better, they did nothing to help her embrace her new surroundings. If anything, they terrified her even more. Looking into the woods surrounding her property and not knowing what lurked just behind the tree line gave her the creeps, but hiking the local trails and actually seeing snakes, alligators, and other critters, some of which she couldn't even identify, brought nightmares.

And yet, here she was....She'd been looking forward to hiking the new trail, but her mind was too cluttered with everything else to focus on enjoying the peaceful morning. She sucked in a shaky breath, the humidity making her chest heavy. "Don't get too far ahead, Thor."

The big, furry dog, who still hadn't quite grown into his chunky paws, stopped at the sound of her voice, turned back to her, and tilted his head, then waited for her to catch up.

"Good boy." She petted his head. "At least, you're having a good time. You sure do love these early morning walks, don't you?"

He dropped his tongue out and panted.

"Come on. There's supposed to be a lake up ahead. I'll get some water out when we get there, and we can rest for a few minutes and have a drink." She hefted her small backpack farther onto her shoulders and started forward.

The trail was becoming more overgrown, the brush encroaching on the open space. When it forked, she hesitated. She'd looked at the map at the edge of the parking lot, but she couldn't remember which way to head. The path to the left held less vegetation and seemed to be used more often, so she turned that way. Most likely, all the trails would converge at the lake anyway, so it probably didn't matter.

A line of sweat trickled down the side of her face. Gia wiped it away, slid an elastic band off her wrist, and tied her hair back. Winter in Florida was a whole lot different from winter in New York. Though she'd be lying to herself if she didn't admit she missed it. The cold bite of winter air—which would freeze her lungs when she inhaled. The beauty of snowflakes falling and blanketing the entire city in white—which would turn to black slush a few days later, leaving puddles of muck scattered wherever she tried to walk, soaking her feet and splashing from tires if she ventured too close to the street. The warmth of a cozy fire and a mug of hot chocolate on the coldest of nights—of course, it wouldn't be the same without someone to cuddle with.

She sighed.

No matter how many times she went over the same arguments in her head, they didn't change the fact she had no clue what she wanted to do. Who knew? Maybe the zoning error would prove to be a blessing in disguise, the shove she needed to return home.

But she had good friends in Boggy Creek, people who'd stood by her and accepted her. And yet when it came right down to it, she still couldn't help feeling like a visitor. New York had always been, and would probably always be, home.

The sound of dried leaves and palm fronds crunching beneath footsteps pulled her from her indecision.

"Thor, come."

Thankfully, he obeyed the command, and she clipped his leash to his collar. He would never hurt anyone, but sometimes he got a little overenthusiastic about greeting new friends, and not everyone appreciated a strange dog, no matter how well meaning, jumping up on them.

"Heel." She kept him close to her side and angled herself so she'd be between him and whoever was coming toward them.

Ahead of her, a stooped figure emerged from the woods and turned onto the trail. The petite woman shuffled toward them—at least, Gia thought it was a woman. It was hard to tell with the flowing, hooded cloak concealing most of her features, but long, salt-and-pepper hair hung limp over the front of her shoulders from beneath the hood. She leaned heavily on a long, thick walking stick that appeared to have been fashioned from an old tree branch.

The woman paused for a moment and shook dried leaves and twigs from her long cloak, then pulled the hood down farther over her face, concealing her features in even deeper shadows.

"Thor, sit." Gia stopped, keeping the puppy close. If he ever jumped on the fragile-looking woman, he'd bowl her over and probably crush her.

As the woman shuffled closer, Thor popped up, tail wagging.

"Thor. Sit." She kept her voice pitched low but tried to make the command strong so he'd know she wasn't playing. Whether or not he'd obey when he got too excited was a toss-up. She wound the leash tighter around her hand, just to be on the safe side.

He dropped back down and looked at her expectantly.

"Good boy." She patted his head.

The woman moved toward them, keeping her head low. When she'd almost reached them, a shadow crossed the path.

A chill raced up Gia's spine, and she shivered and looked up. A dark gray cloud blocked the sun. She was going to have to turn back or pick up the pace a bit. She definitely didn't want to get caught in a torrential downpour in the middle of the forest. She smiled at the woman. "Good morning."

"Good morning, dear." The woman paused and peered at Gia from beneath her hood. Her piercing eyes were the deepest blue Gia had ever seen. Mesmerizing. The woman tilted her head, and the hood shifted, casting a shadow over her eyes and dimming the hypnotic effect. "Might I offer a piece of advice?"

Gia glanced up at the darkening sky again. "Of course."

A frail hand poked out of her long flowing sleeve and landed on Gia's arm. Her ice-cold touch raised goose bumps. "You are headed down the wrong path, dear. You must change course, find another way."

"I...uh..."

The woman patted her hand, then continued on her way.

"Wait… I…" Gia called after her.

The woman didn't even pause, just kept shambling along at the same steady pace.

Gia looked around, unsure whether to continue the way she was headed or turn back. The cloud passed, and the sun reemerged. She looked back over her shoulder.

The woman had already rounded a curve in the trail and disappeared.

Gia shook off a chill. "Weird, huh, Thor?"

Thor tilted his head and studied her, then looked after the woman. Sometimes it freaked her out a little that he seemed to understand her. Then again, she'd never had a dog before, so maybe that was normal.

"Come on, boy." No sense letting the odd encounter stop her from continuing her walk. Besides, maybe the woman hadn't even been talking about the trail she was on. Maybe she'd meant something more mystical. She did seem a bit…eccentric. She kind of reminded Gia of the fortune-teller she'd been talked into visiting at Coney Island one year when she was a teenager, the woman who'd told her she saw a change in her future, something to do with wilderness and a large animal.

Gia and her friends had laughed it off. Born and raised in the heart of New York City, Gia had never entertained the idea of doing anything so exotic. She and her friends had fun trying to guess what it could be, though. Gia had said maybe she would go on a safari in Africa. Addison had thought she'd be a forest ranger and look after bears. Bears…oh…

Gia patted her pocket to make sure her bear spray was there. Yup, right where it was the last hundred times she'd checked. She looked around again at the towering pine trees and thick underbrush. Dark clouds started to gather overhead, unusual for a Florida morning. The storms typically came later in the day, but why take chances? She started forward. "Come on, Thor."

Okay, so maybe she shouldn't be so quick to dismiss the woman's rambling. But what could she have meant? What had Gia been thinking when she'd first encountered the woman? She'd been trying to decide what to do. She'd thought of going back to New York, but she was pretty sure the last thought she'd had before running into the woman involved staying in Florida.

Did that mean she was supposed to leave, after all?

Or maybe her last thought had been about going back home. Her decision to stay or go changed on a minute-by-minute basis. She just couldn't remember.

A squirrel darted across the path; its skinny tail dropped low.

Thor bolted.

Caught off guard, Gia was forced to run along with him, while she desperately tried to free her hand from the tightening leash. "Thor. No. Stop."

Thor bounced into the underbrush, dragging Gia behind him.

She stumbled over an exposed root and went down hard, face-first into a tree trunk.

The squirrel ran up a tree, and Thor jumped up, his front paws landing against the tree trunk, and barked once.

Thankfully, Thor stopping allowed her enough slack to unwind the leash from her hand. She sat up, keeping a tight hold on the leash handle, and gently probed her aching chin. Her fingers came away coated in blood. *Great.* "Thor. Come."

Apparently giving up on the squirrel, Thor trotted over to where she sat. He took one look at her, dropped down to sit, and lowered his head.

Bracing herself against the tree trunk with one hand, Gia climbed to her feet. She stood still, leaning against the tree for a moment, and took a few deep breaths. The throbbing in her face was manageable, so she pushed away from the tree and took a tentative step toward the trail. Her knee buckled, but she regained her footing before taking another spill.

Thor stood and shot her a look from the corner of his eye.

"It's all right, Thor." It really wasn't his fault, just an accident because he was a big dog and got a little overexcited. She patted his head as he fell into step at her side. "Come on, let's just go home."

Once she was back on the trail, she brushed herself off as best she could and hobbled toward the lake. From where she stood, she could see the bridge crossing the lake on the more heavily traveled trail she usually hiked. It should be quicker to skirt along the lake and take the main trail back to the parking lot. With any luck at all, it would be.

She reached the lake and started along the shore, keeping a close watch on the water for any sign of movement. She slid her hand into her pocket and clutched the canister of bear spray.

Soft muck sucked at her sneakers. A loud sucking sound accompanied each step. Maybe she just wasn't cut out for hiking. Of course, paddleboarding hadn't worked out much better. Everything had been going well, until she'd seen a log in the water and realized it had eyes.

A mosquito landed on her arm, and she swatted it away. Another took its place. She slapped an itch on her face, then gasped at the sting. She'd forgotten about the scrapes she must have sustained when she'd hit the tree. Her back started to itch, and she shifted Thor's leash to the other hand so she could reach it.

The puppy lurched ahead.

"Thor, no."

He shot a look over his shoulder at her and stopped, then turned in a circle and whimpered.

A pang of guilt shot through her. Maybe she should have done more to reassure him the mishap hadn't been his fault. "It's okay, boy."

She reached out to pet him, and he whined again and turned in another circle.

"What's wrong, Thor?" She petted his head. "Come on, let's—"

As she rounded a large tree, she almost tripped over something half-submerged in the muck. She yanked out the bear spray and held it out in front of her, then crept closer.

A woman's body lay facedown in the mud. Even though her upper body lay half in the marshy underbrush, Gia recognized the woman's clothing. She was still wearing the same hot pink dress she'd worn the day before when she'd come into the café. One sandal had come off but remained tied around her ankle. The other foot was submerged in the murky water, so Gia couldn't tell if she was still wearing the other shoe. Unless someone else shared Marcia's tacky taste in clothing, it was a pretty safe bet she'd just stumbled over the council president.

He lapped greedily. Apparently, his stomach was in better shape than hers.

A black SUV stopped a little ways from where she sat on the log. A man emerged and slammed the door shut. Despite his jeans and T-shirt, Gia had no trouble recognizing Captain Hayes. *Oh, boy.* The universe really was conspiring against her today.

Ignoring the others, who'd gathered in a semicircle a few feet away, Hayes homed in on Gia, frowned, and strode toward her.

Great.

"Ms. Morelli." He propped his hands on his hips and stared down at her. "Would you care to tell me what happened?"

Gia bristled. Who did he think he was? She surged to her feet, and an eddy of darkness encroached. She shot a hand out to steady herself against a tree, then waited a few seconds for her head to clear. "I was hiking the trail with Thor, and I found a woman's body."

"Mmm-hmm… And is this body any relation to you?"

She bit back the nasty response that formed in her mind an instant before it could pop out of her mouth. "No."

Not exactly.

He was bound to find out there was a connection, but let him figure that out for himself.

She was saved from having to elaborate by the arrival of a second officer. Officer Leo Dumont hurried toward her. "Are you okay? What happened? Did someone hurt you?"

"I'm all right, thank you." She glared at Hayes. At least Leo had thought to ask if she was hurt. "I just fell."

He touched her chin lightly and tilted her head to examine her face more closely. "Your cheek is just scraped, but it looks like your chin might need a few stitches. Do you want an ambulance, or should I just have Savannah pick you up and take you to the hospital?"

Gia had no intention of going to the hospital. She just wanted the interrogation she was sure Hayes was set on over with so she could go home. "I'm fine. Really. Thanks, Leo. I have some butterfly bandages in my first aid kit. Right now, I just want to answer whatever questions you guys have and go home."

Leo held her gaze, staring into her eyes. "Are you sure? These wounds need to be cleaned out good, or you'll get an infection."

"Positive. I'll take care of it, thank you."

Captain Hayes watched the exchange, arms folded across his chest. "Can you show me where the body is?"

Gia started to turn, but Bryce grabbed her arm. "I can show him. Why don't you sit down?"

"Thank you."

Hayes studied her another moment before following Bryce down the trail and around the curved shore.

Gia sat back on the stump.

Leo squatted down in front of her, his face lined with concern. "What happened, Gia?"

"I had my hand wrapped in Thor's leash, and he took off after a squirrel. Before I could loosen the leash, I tripped over a root and fell."

"You're sure you're okay?"

She offered a small smile. "I'm fine. Just tired and sore."

His blue eyes twinkled. "You know that's going to be funny later, right?"

"Yeah, but right now is too soon."

Leo smirked but his eyes remained somber; then he turned away as another police vehicle arrived.

Detective Hunter Quinn jumped out of his jeep and strode toward them. "What happened? Are you okay?"

Leo stood. "She's fine. She just fell."

Hunt stopped and examined her face, then frowned. "Don't even tell me you found her?"

She nodded. Though she was relieved to have Hunt there, she'd hoped for a more personal greeting, maybe even a little comfort.

Hunt looked back over his shoulder and pointed at the black SUV blocking the trail. "What's Hayes doing here?"

"Said he was camping with his son in the forest when the call came in," Leo said. "Didn't you catch his radio transmission?"

"I was close by, but I wasn't in my truck. I only caught the original call. Where is he?"

Leo gestured toward the trail that led around the lake.

Hunt sighed and looked at Gia. "Are you sure you're all right?"

"Positive."

He nodded once and then took off after Hayes.

Gia watched him go. "Is he okay?"

"What do you mean?" Leo asked.

"I don't know.... He seems a bit distant lately."

"I hadn't noticed."

Gia let it go. Maybe Hunt was only acting distant with *her*. The thought didn't sit well, but what could she do? As far as she knew, she hadn't done anything to make him pull away. Not that there was much to pull away from. Maybe she'd simply read more into their friendship than there really was.

Raised voices intruded on her pity party.

Bryce emerged from the trail and rejoined his friends.

"I'll be right back." Leo patted her hand, then stood and headed toward Bryce.

Gia started toward the trail. Whatever was going on down there, she wanted to know. The sound of Hunt and Captain Hayes yelling at each other reached her before she even left the clearing. Maybe she should back off and let them go at it without her eavesdropping. Or maybe they weren't yelling at each other. She glanced down at Thor standing beside her, then rounded the curve into the trail with him at her side. As soon as she could see the men through the trees, she stopped. No sense alerting them to her presence.

"I already said no." Captain Hayes stood facing Hunt, red-faced, his finger against Hunt's chest.

"But—" Hunt stood his ground, jaw clenched. If his rigid posture was any indication, he was just as angry as his captain.

"No buts. I don't want to hear it."

Hunt took a step back and shoved a hand through his dark hair. "We have to search the house as soon as possible."

Captain Hayes stepped toward him, obviously unwilling to let the matter go. "I am not kidding, Detective. If you go anywhere near that woman's house without a search warrant"—he gestured toward Marcia Steers—"you will be off the force so fast you won't know what happened."

Hunt leaned closer until he was face-to-face with Captain Hayes, then spoke through gritted teeth. "You don't know she was killed here. Right now, we have just cause to search the deceased's home without the warrant."

Gia held her breath. She thought briefly of interrupting, not because she didn't want to see Captain Hayes get decked, but because she didn't want to see Hunt get into trouble.

"Look, Detective Quinn, the medical examiner hasn't even arrived yet. I'll make a determination about the warrant after he examines the body. And I'm warning you, you'd better not run off half-cocked and do anything stupid."

"As the lead detective on this case, it's within my rights to decide—"

Hayes held up a hand to stop him. "If you were the lead detective on the case, it would be your decision, but you're not."

"What!" Hunt exploded.

"As of this minute, you are no longer assigned to this case. In any capacity. Now leave, or I will have you escorted off my crime scene."

"You can't do that."

"I just did."

"On what grounds?"

Gia started forward. If someone didn't step between these two, they were going to end up brawling.

"Your relationship with the deceased. Everyone knows you two were hot and heavy until Ms. Steers strayed," Captain Hayes blurted. "And don't think it's escaped anyone's attention that the two of you have been sneaking around again."

His words stopped her dead in her tracks. Apparently, it had escaped her attention, but it certainly explained Hunt's behavior of late.

Hunt shoved the captain.

He stumbled back but regained his footing before he could fall into the swampy wetlands and yanked his radio from his belt. "That's it. You're out of here. Now."

Hunt turned and stalked away before Captain Hayes could call for help. Gia froze.

When Hunt reached her standing on the trail, his gaze met hers. He held their stare for a moment, then continued down the trail without saying a word.

Momentarily shocked at the anger in his eyes, Gia stood and watched him storm off. Then she hurried after him.

A group of officers and a short man with glasses and a black suit blocked her path as they made their way toward the crime scene.

When she was forced to step aside to allow them room to pass, Hunt rounded a bend in the trail, and she lost sight of him.

Thor fidgeted wildly at her side, getting himself tangled in the leash.

"It's okay, boy." She unwrapped the leash from between his legs, then weaved her fingers into his thick fur and waited. No matter how badly she wanted to reach Hunt, or how rattled she'd been by Captain Hayes's accusation, she wasn't going anywhere until the crime scene techs passed.

Leo trailed behind the group. He stopped as soon as he spotted her. "There you are. I've been looking everywhere for you."

"Sorry, I uh…" She what? Was eavesdropping on Hunt and his captain arguing? Her head was reeling too badly to think straight. "Wanted to see what was happening."

"Yeah, well, until we have a better idea of what's going on, I don't want you wandering around out here alone."

"I'm not alone. Thor is with me."

"Gia. You know what I mean."

"Fine. I won't wander around anymore. I promise." *Not like there's anything left to see here anyway.* But she couldn't help but wonder what had Hunt acting so strangely. If he was really seeing the woman who now lay at the edge of the swamp, her heart ached for him. At least, it did when her anger receded for a moment.

"Come on." With a hand on her elbow, Leo gently guided her back toward the clearing. "I still need to ask you some questions, then I can have Savannah pick you up if you want."

"Actually, my car is in the main parking lot at the front of the park. Would you mind just dropping me off there?"

"No problem." He led her back to the log she'd been sitting on when he'd arrived.

Bryce and his friends were nowhere to be found. Apparently, the police had finished questioning them and sent them on their way.

"Now, tell me what happened."

"I already told you—"

He held up a hand to stop her and pulled out a notepad and pen. "From the beginning. Just walk me through everything."

Gia sighed, resigned to spending a while longer in the mosquito-infested forest, and swatted a bug off her forearm. A small lizard darted up the log beside her, then launched himself onto a bush.

She needed to get this over with and go home. "I was walking Thor down one of the trails over there...." She gestured in the direction of the trail she'd been following. "Thor ran after a squirrel and I fell. I was going to turn back, but I realized I was almost to the lake and thought it would be quicker to head back on the main trail. All I wanted to do was hurry up and get home."

Leo nodded but obviously didn't take the hint since he simply waited, pen poised over his pad.

"When I reached the lake, I started along the edge of the water. That's when I tripped over the body. I screamed, and Bryce came running over and called the police."

"Did you see anyone else?"

"Not until later, after I left the trail and sat down here. Then I saw Bryce's friends and a few stragglers who must have shown up when they heard the commotion."

"I found it in my desk drawer. Do you think Marcia could have put it in there yesterday?"

"I guess. I saw her go through the door to the office, so it was only a matter of a minute or two before I met up with her, but I suppose she'd have had time to drop this in the drawer, especially if it was already written." Savannah frowned down at the paper. "What do you think it means?"

"I have no idea. She didn't mention any documents to me yesterday."

"Hmm..."

"What?"

"I'm just wondering if she didn't want to talk in front of me specifically."

"What difference would that make?"

"I'm not sure," Savannah said. "But my brother does sit on the council, and if the documents are regarding the zoning error, she may not have wanted to take a chance on anyone from the council finding out."

"I guess. But what kind of documents could she be talking about?"

"I have no idea, but Tommy called back a little while ago, and he said Marcia seemed to be the person most intent on shutting you down. At least, at first. He said lately she's been pretty quiet on the subject."

"Huh..."

"Yeah. It doesn't make much sense for her to be so set on closing you down, then want to give you documents that would help you stay open."

"No, it doesn't." But it definitely seemed Marcia wanted something with her.

Savannah snapped her fingers. "Wait. Maybe she was going to blackmail you?"

"Blackmail?"

"You know, she tries to get the café shut down, then offers a way to keep it open if you pay her."

"I don't know. Why would she do that?" Savannah could be right; Marcia had seemed nervous. Then again, Captain Hayes had said Hunt and Marcia had rekindled their relationship. Maybe Marcia was trying to close her down so she'd run back to New York. Or maybe she'd invited Gia to her house so she'd walk in on the two of them together. Either scenario would be a good way to eliminate the competition.

"Who knows." Savannah perched on the edge of the desk. "Maybe she needed the money."

"Or maybe the documents have nothing to do with keeping the café open. Maybe it's paperwork to shut it down."

"Maybe, but then why all the subterfuge?"

Gia's thoughts bounced back to Hunt. What could his involvement be? Gia wanted to ask if he'd been acting strange lately, but the last thing she wanted to do was ping Savannah's radar. She was in no mood to answer a million questions about their seemingly nonexistent relationship. "Hunt was arguing with the captain at the crime scene."

"What about?" She turned Marcia's note over and studied the back.

"Searching Marcia's house. Hunt wanted to search, but Captain Hayes said he had to wait for a warrant."

"So?"

"That's just it. I have no idea, but Hunt was hell-bent on getting into that house as soon as possible. Do you think he could know something about whatever she was doing?"

"I don't know. I guess it's possible." Savannah apparently gave up on the note and tossed it onto Gia's desk. "Did Hunt get his way?"

"Nope. The captain took him off the case and told him to leave."

Savannah's eyes widened. "Seriously? I wonder why. Those two go at it all the time, and I've never seen Hayes do anything that drastic before."

Gia tried for a nonchalant shrug, but it probably came off looking more like a twitch. "He said it was because Hunt was involved with Marcia."

Savannah's gaze shot to hers.

So much for not pinging her radar. Heat flared in Gia's cheeks. "He said the whole town knew about their bad breakup when Hunt found Marcia cheating on him."

Savannah leaned over and patted Gia's clasped hands.

Dang. She'd seen right through her. As usual.

"It was a long time ago, Gia. Before you moved here. And believe me, it was nothing serious. Hunt doesn't believe in seeing anyone else while you're dating, even casually."

"He said everyone knew they'd rekindled their relationship." She lowered her gaze, so Savannah wouldn't catch the pain in her eyes.

If she did, she let it drop. "Well, whatever documents she had, if they are related to the zoning, there should be a copy on file at the records building downtown."

"You think?"

"I don't see why not. All of the zoning information should be public record."

Gia shoved her chair back, stood, and grabbed her purse. "Do you have time to take a ride?"

"You bet, but only if you promise to buy me lunch after we're done."

"It's a deal." It took less than fifteen minutes to drive around the park and lake and reach the area of Boggy Creek Savannah referred to as downtown. Unlike the quaint, old-fashioned Main Street, the downtown area boasted several contemporary office parks. The records building sat in the same complex with the police station, and though she scanned the lot for his jeep, she saw no sign of Hunt.

"Everything okay?" Savannah shifted the car into park and glanced over at her. "You're uncharacteristically quiet."

"I'm fine. I guess I just have a lot on my mind." She climbed out of the car before Savannah could question her further.

She had no desire to explain how she'd been having second thoughts about staying in Boggy Creek, or even worse, that she'd thought she and Hunt had been moving toward some kind of relationship before he'd backed off. Savannah was Gia's best friend, and she had no doubt Savannah would go to bat for her with Hunt. But Hunt was Savannah's family, and Gia had no intention of saying anything that might cause a rift between them. Better to let the matter drop, at least until she had some idea about what was going on with him.

They entered the cool lobby, and Gia shivered. "Why do they keep the air-conditioning on so high everywhere down here?"

"Because it's so hot out." Savannah smirked and dropped her keys and purse into a tray, then strode through the metal detector.

Gia followed.

Once the guard searched their purses and handed them back, they walked down a long corridor. Gia checked her phone for the time. "Do you think they'll be out to lunch?"

"Probably not yet." Savannah reached the end of the hallway and pulled open an unmarked door.

A short, stocky woman with dark hair pulled into a bun looked up from the paperwork scattered across her desk. "Can I—oh, hey, Savannah. What's up?"

"Hi, Molly. How have you been?"

"Good, and you?"

"Can't complain." Savannah gestured toward Gia. "This is my friend, Gia. She opened the All-Day Breakfast Café in town."

Molly stood and reached across her desk to shake Gia's hand. "It's nice to meet you, Gia. I've eaten at the café a few times, and I love it. Your home fries are amazing."

Gia shook her hand and smiled. Maybe if she wasn't stuck in the kitchen all the time, she'd have already met Molly. "Thank you."

"So, I take it this isn't a social call. What can I help you with?" Molly propped her glasses on top of her head.

"We were wondering if it's possible to check all of the records related to a specific address," Savannah said.

"Sure. What's the address?"

"1012 Main Street."

Gia held her breath while Molly closed the folder she'd been working on and set it aside in favor of her computer. Could it really be that easy to find out what they needed?

Molly put her glasses back on and typed in the address. "Okay, let see. The house was originally built in the late 1800s, so a lot of the history was never put on the computer, but we should have the tax and sales history, at the least."

"What about the zoning history?"

"Probably." Molly smiled. "Though I can't make any promises."

Gia envisioned boxes of paperwork piled high in a warehouse somewhere. "Is there a way to access it?"

"Yup. The old-fashioned way." Molly stood and grabbed a set of keys from a hook, then held open a swinging door that led toward the back of the office. "Follow me."

She led them into a huge room filled with file cabinets.

Okay, a little less daunting than Gia had imagined, but not much. "How are we supposed to find anything in here?"

"The actual records aren't on a digital file, but we do keep a computerized catalogue of where to find them." Molly looked something up on a computer sitting on a battered desk near the door, then headed deeper into the maze of file cabinets with Gia and Savannah on her heels. When she reached the row she was looking for, she opened a drawer and sorted through a number of manila folders. She pulled one out and opened it, then paused. "Wait a minute. That's not right."

"What's wrong?" Gia looked over her shoulder at the empty manila folder she held open.

She put the folder down on top of the file cabinet, went through the folders in the drawer again, then opened the drawers above and below it and skimmed through their contents. "You're not allowed to remove records from this building, and yet they seem to be gone."

"What do you mean?" Gia asked.

"I mean, they're not here."

Savannah picked up the folder from the top of the cabinet and studied a paper stapled to the front of it. She paled, and her finger shook as she pointed to the page. "What is this?"

"The signature page. It contains a list of people who have signed out the folder," Molly answered, distracted as she searched through the file cabinet once again. "But you're only allowed to look at them here. You can't take them with you."

Savannah's expression went completely blank. She dropped the folder back onto the cabinet, turned, and walked out without another word.

"Savannah?" Gia called after her.

She kept walking without even looking back, then shoved through the door.

Gia picked up the folder and looked at the page. A list of printed names followed by signatures and dates. The last name recorded was Marcia Steers, who'd signed the folder out a week prior to being killed.

"Do you know what Marcia wanted with the folder?" Gia asked.

"No, I'm sorry. I wasn't here when she signed it out." Molly slammed the file cabinet closed, then stormed off muttering to herself.

Gia tossed the folder on top of the cabinet and started to turn, but the name before Marcia's caught her attention. Howard Hayes. Captain Hayes? She ran her finger along the line until she came to the date. Twenty years ago? What would Hayes have wanted with this information twenty years ago?

Another name jumped off the page. Sara Mills. Mills? The same last name as Savannah. Were they related? Was that why Savannah had acted so strangely? She checked the date. It seemed Sara had signed the folder out twenty years ago as well, only one week before Hayes. And someone named Sean McNeil signed it out two days after Sara. What was so important about this folder twenty years ago?

She pulled out her phone and snapped a picture of the list, which only contained one other name. A Floyd Masters had signed the folder out a month before Sara Mills. Leaving the folder where it was, Gia shoved her phone back into her purse and went after Savannah. It was time for some answers.

Chapter 5

Gia hurried across the parking lot to Savannah's car and found her sitting behind the wheel, staring out the windshield with the air-conditioning turned all the way up. She slid into the passenger seat.

A million questions barreled through her mind, begging for attention, the most pressing of which was, "Are you okay, Savannah?"

She shook her head and adjusted the vent until the cold air ruffled her hair. "I don't know."

"Is the Howard Hayes from the list Captain Hayes?"

"Yes." She sucked in a deep breath, then blew it out slowly. "And Sara Mills is my mother."

Shock slammed through Gia like a punch in the gut. "Your mother?"

"Yes. Apparently she signed that same folder out just days before she was killed."

Gia adjusted the vent on her side, letting the cool air wash over her. "And Hayes signed it out a week later."

"Seems so." She finally looked at Gia. "Just days after she was killed."

Gia didn't know what to say to comfort Savannah. When they'd lived together in New York, Savannah had mentioned that her mother had passed away when she was young, but until recently, Savannah hadn't even told Gia her mother had been murdered. And she still hadn't mentioned being the one to find her. If not for Hunt, Gia still wouldn't know that part of the story.

The memory of Hunt arguing with Captain Hayes flashed through Gia's mind. "Do you think Hunt knows?"

"I don't know. Maybe, but I don't see what difference it makes."

"Hunt wanted to get into that house awfully badly. I wonder why." Gia pursed her lips and waited for Savannah's line of thought to catch up to hers.

"What do you think he's looking for?"

"I don't know. He never said, but once he does search, whatever documents Marcia wanted to give me might be gone." Another thought begged for attention. "Plus, Captain Hayes threw Hunt off the case, and now Hayes is in charge, and well..." She didn't have to remind Savannah his name was listed on the paperwork right after Sara Mills.

"And Captain Hayes, who was a detective back then, screwed up the investigation into my mother's murder pretty badly. I know what you must want to do."

"What are you talking about?"

"Don't play innocent with me, Gia. I know you too well."

Gia smiled. She was right. Sometimes Savannah knew what she was thinking even before she did. But not this time. The idea of checking out Marcia's house had begun to niggle at her the instant she'd found out who Sara Mills was. "So... Do you want to help me?"

"Help you what? Break into Marcia's house?"

"No. Not exactly."

Savannah held her stare.

"Okay, yes. I just want to take a peek and see if I can find what she was talking about in the letter. If Hayes did have anything to do with what happened to your mother, once he gets into that house, any evidence will be gone forever."

"Are you out of your mind?"

"No, listen. Hunt is off the case, which means Captain Hayes is in charge. And Hayes hates me. If Marcia had something I could use to keep the café open, Hayes would probably dump it in the trash first chance he got. And that's the best-case scenario. If that paperwork has anything to do with him bungling your mother's case, he'll probably burn it."

"Well, I can't really argue that, since you're probably right. But still. If he finds us in there, we'll be in jail for sure. Or worse, he'll tell Hunt."

"So we'll have to make sure he doesn't catch us. Besides, I still have the letter Marcia left in my desk. Technically, we're not breaking in since I was invited."

Savannah shook her head and started the car. "Marcia was pretty insistent they were closing the café. What makes you think she had anything that would help you?"

"At this point, anything might help. Even knowing if the property was always zoned residential might be useful. You never know."

Deep lines bracketed Savannah's mouth as she shifted into gear and pulled out of the parking lot, though Gia didn't know if it was the thought of breaking and entering, concern about getting caught, or confusion over whatever involvement her mother had with the café that weighed on her so heavily. Probably a bit of everything.

"Swing by the café for a minute. I just want to grab something."

"What?"

Gia grinned. "Gloves."

Savannah laughed and shook her head. "You're going to have us in jail. You know that, right?"

"Nope. Not a chance. That's what the gloves are for. Hopefully no one will ever know we were there." *Including Detective Tall, Dark, and Nosy.*

Savannah made a quick detour past the café.

Gia ran in for two pairs of rubber dishwashing gloves, then jumped back into the car. "Do you know what the café was twenty years ago?"

"The building sat empty for a long time before you opened the café. Last I remember before that it was a bar, but that had to close down."

"Why?"

"Originally, it was a nice bar and restaurant where people went to relax and have a drink, maybe some appetizers. Parents could even bring their kids to sit at the tables and have something to eat. My parents brought us a few times. But then the clientele started to change, got rougher, meaner. It reached the point where no one else would go in." Savannah hit the turn signal, then checked her rearview mirror before switching lanes and making a left onto a narrow road. "The cops were in there breaking up fights multiple times a night. It was a mess. Until someone, maybe the council, eventually managed to shut them down."

"How'd they do that?"

"I don't remember. I was just a kid at the time."

"It's been empty that long?" Gia asked.

"Ha ha."

"I didn't mean—"

Savannah shot her a grin. "Why do you think it was so cheap?"

Savannah slowed as she passed a small cottage surrounded by woods on three sides but didn't stop. A row of hedges crossed the front of the property with an opening just wide enough for the driveway.

Luckily for Gia, Marcia Steers apparently liked her privacy.

"Where do you want me to park?" Savannah asked, as she continued toward the end of the block.

"I don't know this area well. Can we park on the street behind the house and cut through the woods?"

"There's no street behind the house, only a nature preserve."

Gia looked over her shoulder at the quiet residential block. Marcia's neighbors seemed just as interested in their privacy as she was in hers. Many of the houses boasted hedge walls or fences with gates. "Do you think anyone will notice if we just park in the driveway?"

Savannah stopped at a stop sign on the corner and waited. "I doubt the neighbors would think much about a car in the driveway. They probably haven't yet heard she passed away, but who knows how long the police will be able to keep it quiet."

"If past experience is any indication, it's probably all over town by now."

"True." Savannah hit the turn signal and made a left. "We'll park on the next street over and just walk around the block. This way if anyone shows up to search, we can go out the back, cut through the woods and across the street, and circle back around to the car. Besides, chances are, anyone coming to search would come in from the main road."

She was glad Savannah was at least thinking clearly, because all Gia really cared about at that moment was getting into that house. "Sounds good."

Once they parked, Gia resisted the urge to run toward the house. No sense drawing attention to themselves. She and Savannah strolled casually down the street and around the block. Neither of them said anything. Gia's thoughts were too chaotic to focus on conversation; the events of the past few days weighed heavily upon her. Fear of getting caught hammered at her, and she just wanted to be done and get out of there.

Once they started up the driveway and the hedges offered at least some cover, she was more able to concentrate. She handed Savannah a pair of gloves and pulled on her own. "How are we going to get in?"

"I don't know yet." Savannah pulled on her gloves and looked around as they climbed the steps to the front porch. "But the note said there was a spare key on the porch."

Even though Marcia wasn't married, Gia didn't want to take any chances. She pressed the doorbell and waited.

Savannah lifted a flowerpot and looked underneath; then she peeked under all the cushions on the wicker chairs and love seat.

When no one came to the door, Gia joined her searching the wraparound porch. She hit the jackpot with the third planter she checked. She lifted a fake rock out of the planter and held it out to Savannah. "I found it."

"Okay, let's hurry."

She opened the false bottom and removed the key, then looked up and down the street once more. All quiet. It was now or never. She unlocked the door, opened it, and poked her head in. "Hello?"

"Anything?" Savannah whispered from right behind her.

"No." She entered the foyer and held the door for Savannah, then glanced around the street once more before shutting the door. "Let's split up. Her note said the documents would be on the table, but it didn't say which one. I'll start in the kitchen."

"I'll look for a desk or an office or something."

The kitchen didn't take long to search. A frying pan filled with water was soaking in the sink, and a plate containing half an omelet sat on the table beside a half-empty glass of orange juice and a full cup of coffee. She felt the cups. Both were room temperature, so she had no idea whether Marcia's breakfast had been interrupted that morning. Perhaps she'd left her breakfast and run out the day before in her haste to see Gia. Though that didn't seem likely, she couldn't rule it out either, since Marcia had still been wearing the same clothes she'd worn to the café the day before when Gia had found her at the lake.

A quick search of the rest of the kitchen came up empty. Other than a Post-it pad, which she flipped through and found blank, there wasn't another piece of paper in the kitchen.

Giving up, she headed to the living room and found Savannah hunched over a small desk. "Anything?"

Savannah shoved the center drawer shut. "Nothing. A stack of bills, a few receipts, and a cookbook. That's about it."

"Did you look for an office?"

"Yes. She doesn't have one. One of the spare bedrooms is a guest room and the other a workout room."

"Did you look through the master bedroom?"

Savannah shook her head. "Not yet."

"All right, let's do that and then get out of here. Snooping around a dead woman's house is starting to give me the creeps." *Not to mention a major case of guilt.*

She followed Savannah to the master bedroom at the end of the hall. Dust motes floated in the sunlight streaming through the window. A frilly pink bedspread lay smooth over the bed, throw pillows arranged neatly along the headboard. So Marcia had time to make the bed before breakfast. If she'd slept in it, at least. Could be she'd stayed over…somewhere else. Maybe that's why she still had on the same outfit.

Savannah pulled out one drawer after another, rummaging through the clothes, then shutting them and moving on. "There's nothing here."

Gia felt along the top shelf of the closet, searched through an assortment of shoe boxes, all containing strappy sandals with stiletto heels. The woman sure had a thing for shoes. She flipped through the pages of a few photo albums, what appeared to be vacation photos, skimmed through a couple of paperbacks on the nightstand, then gave up.

"I can't find anything either." She stood in the center of the room and looked around. They had to have missed something. She thought of the boxes and boxes of paperwork she'd had in the garage when she'd first moved into her house. There were still boxes there she had no clue what to do with. "How can anyone have so little paperwork?"

Savannah pursed her lips and looked around. "It doesn't seem possible. I think we must be looking in the wrong place."

Gia dropped to her knees and lifted the corner of the bedspread. "Anything?"

"I don't know." She reached under and pulled out a shoe box. "Probably just another pair of shoes."

Savannah sat on the edge of the bed.

Gia lifted the lid. "Bingo."

"You found them?"

"I'm not sure, but there are papers in here. Do you think we should just take the whole thing?"

"Let's just see what it is quick. If it relates to the café, we'll take it and get out of here. Otherwise, you can just put it back where you found it."

"Okay." She sat next to Savannah on the bed and set the shoe box between them. The first envelope Gia opened contained a letter from someone named Hank, proclaiming his desire for Marcia in way more explicit detail than Gia needed to know. "Well, I wish I hadn't read that."

Gia put the letter back in the envelope and set it aside. The next envelope held a stack of pictures—Marcia and Hunt at the beach, a theme park, in the woods, in front of Hunt's jeep, both smiling, Hunt's arm usually slung around her shoulder.

Savannah took the pictures from her and slipped them back into the envelope. "It was a long time ago, Gia."

She shrugged, but she didn't try to deny the hurt. "Whatever. It's not like Hunt and I were seeing each other or anything."

"Come on." Savannah reached across the box and held Gia's hand. "We both know you and Hunt were headed toward a relationship. Heck, you probably still are. Hunt never really got too serious with a woman, but he didn't cheat either. If he was seeing someone, he wouldn't fool around with anyone else. Even if he wasn't quite sure where the relationship was headed, I've never once known him to sneak around."

Gia couldn't deny the bit of relief Savannah's words brought. Maybe Hunt just needed time. Maybe he just had a lot going on. She'd almost reached the bottom of the stack of papers, and they still hadn't come across anything related to the café or any other zoning issues. It seemed the box contained only personal items, and another pang of guilt shot through Gia at the thought of intruding on Marcia's privacy.

Savannah opened the last envelope and shuffled through what appeared to be a pile of pictures. When she'd almost reached the bottom of the pile, she gasped.

"What? Did you find something?"

"I found something, all right." She glanced up, put the stack of pictures back together, and held it out to Gia.

Gia took them from her and started to shuffle through them. Marcia dressed in skimpy lingerie, in several compromising poses. "Any special reason you're sharing these with me?"

"Just keep going."

She looked through a couple more pictures, then stopped when she came to one of Marcia and a man. She was still wearing the same sheer nightie, and the picture appeared to be a selfie of the two of them sitting on Marcia's bed. "Is that who I think it is?"

"Yup. Turn it over."

Me and Hank was scribbled on the back of the photo in black ink, followed by what she assumed was the date the picture was taken. "This was just taken a few weeks ago."

"It seems so."

"Oh my gosh. Marcia was having an affair with Maybelle's husband."

The sound of a car door slamming cut through her shock.

Chapter 6

Gia lurched to her feet. "Did you hear that?"

"Hear what?" Savannah started hurriedly putting things back into the box.

Another car door slammed, followed by the muffled sound of a man's voice.

"Uh-oh." Savannah stared at her for a moment, eyes wide, then jumped up, frantically shoved the remaining items into the box, and slammed the top back on.

"Wait," Gia whispered and held up the stack of pictures. "What about these?"

Savannah grabbed them and snatched one from the pile, then lifted the corner of the lid, stuffed the rest into the box, and shoved it under the bed.

Gia stood beside the bed, her gaze darting back and forth between the window and the open bedroom door. "What do we do? Go out the window?" she whispered.

A door squeaked as it opened.

She froze. "Oh, man. We forgot to lock the front door."

"You don't have to do this, you know." An all-too-familiar voice floated down the hallway.

"I know, but I'm here now, so..."

Savannah grabbed Gia's arm and yanked her to the floor, then shoved her toward the bed. "Get under. Hurry."

Gia shoved the shoe box out of the way and slid beneath the bed far enough to allow Savannah room to slip in beside her. With her head toward the foot of the bed, Gia could just make out a sliver of the wood floor in the hallway.

One set of work boots and one set of shiny black men's dress shoes walked toward them.

"They've got to be somewhere, and I didn't see anything in the woods."

"If she had them with her, they're probably gone now. You know that, Hunt."

Hunt sighed. "Yeah, I do. But she was scared, Leo. Really scared."

"I'm sorry."

"I know." His voice was husky, filled with emotion. "I have to find whoever did this."

An ache formed in Gia's chest, and it had nothing to do with fear of getting caught.

"We will. Now let's find the papers and get out of here before Captain Hayes shows up with his search warrant."

Hunt made a sound somewhere between a grunt and a snort, then headed for the nearest dresser.

Drawers opened and closed; then the closet door slid open. Gia kept track of their shoes and footsteps as best she could, but it was hopeless. Sooner or later, they were going to look under the bed. Unless they found what they were looking for. Hope surged for a fraction of a second but plummeted just as quickly. She and Savannah had already searched everywhere. There were no documents to be found. She lowered her head onto her folded hands and awaited her fate.

Something moved in her peripheral vision. She tilted her head to get a better view.

A small black spider crawled across the bottom of the footboard toward her. If she weren't so deathly afraid of spiders, it probably wouldn't have been that big a deal. As it was, it took every ounce of her willpower to keep from screaming like a banshee and fleeing the room.

She covered her mouth with her hands to stifle the scream and tried to scoot backward away from the oncoming creature.

The spider dropped off the bed, dangling from a web strand inches from her face.

Gia jerked up and smacked the back of her head on the underside of the bed.

Savannah grabbed her arm and dug her nails into Gia's flesh. Hard.

Someone cleared his throat.

Gia tried to refocus on keeping track of Hunt and Leo. In her moment of arachnophobic panic, she'd lost track of them. It was no use. Not much else existed for her in that moment other than the small, creepy spider inching his way closer to her. She cringed farther back.

lately. I admit he hasn't been around much, and when he is, he seems distant and kind of cold, but I'd be really surprised if he was seeing anyone else."

Gia didn't have the strength to deal with another man cheating on her. "It's not like we're dating or anything. More like friends, really. Family, almost. He's free to do whatever he wants."

Savannah's gaze intensified. "Hunt has feelings for you, Gia. He's just taking it slow because he knows what you've been through. He understands how hard it is for you to trust him, or anyone. He'll never push you, but he won't move ahead until you can trust him. At least more than you do now."

Gia picked at the chipped red polish on her thumbnail, trying to hide her pain from Savannah. Probably a waste of time. "Did Hunt actually say that?"

"He didn't have to."

"So you really don't believe he was seeing Marcia?"

"Nope. I think something strange is going on, but not that."

"Do you think Hank Sanford is involved somehow?"

Savannah studied her for a moment but, thankfully, accepted the change of subject. "I guess it's possible. Everyone knows Maybelle's meaner than a sack full of rattlesnakes, and she's the kinder of the two."

"Maybe Maybelle found out?" But even if she did, would she have killed Marcia for cheating with Hank? It didn't seem likely, but Gia really didn't know Maybelle all that well. Quite honestly, Gia doubted Maybelle had the ambition to kill anyone.

"Could be." Savannah sat up straighter. "Anyway, I gotta run. I promised my dad I'd be home to make dinner tonight."

"I thought Joey was supposed to cook."

"He was, but he's got a date."

"Convenient." Gia laughed as she opened the door and climbed out. Savannah's youngest brother would do just about anything to get out of cooking.

"Exactly. And don't think I forgot you owe me lunch one of these days." Savannah winked, then waved as she pulled away.

Gia watched her drive down the road, then fished the keys out of her bag and turned toward the café. The warm Florida sun beat against her back, and she tilted her face up toward the heat and sighed. Fluffy white clouds dotted the brilliant blue sky, a far cry from the usual gray winter sky in New York. She needed to get the ad for a cook finished, but most everything else was done. Nothing that couldn't wait until morning. If she was going to live in Florida, she may as well take advantage of the gorgeous weather.

Dropping the keys back into her bag, she headed down the semi-crowded sidewalk toward the doggie day care center to pick up Thor. She'd take him home, give him an early dinner, then maybe take a walk through her development. On the road. Not in the woods.

Several people greeted her as she walked, some saying hello, others simply waving. She enjoyed the sense of community living in a small town brought, and she was beginning to recognize familiar faces, even though she hadn't really made more than a handful of friends. The atmosphere was so much more relaxed than the hectic pace of living in New York. But while she appreciated the more peaceful pace, she had a hard time slowing down, too used to doing everything at a hundred miles an hour to be completely comfortable moving any slower. Even when her mind tried, her body refused to cooperate.

That feeling of peace would be short lived, though. Once people found out Marcia had been killed, an undercurrent of fear and uncertainty would taint the harmony. A buzz would fill the air as parents watched their children more closely, normally friendly locals became just a bit warier of strangers, and expressions turned more serious when people gathered at the local gossip hot spots. Unfortunately, in Boggy Creek, a town that normally had an extremely low violent crime rate, Gia had seen it happen before.

"Gia."

She paused and looked over her shoulder.

"Wait up." Trevor, who owned the ice cream parlor down the street from the cafe, glanced both ways, then hurried across the street toward her.

She waved and waited for him to catch up. Trevor was one of the few people who'd become a good friend since she'd arrived. Though they'd started out with a date of sorts, they quickly came to realize they were better as friends. Since the feeling was mutual, there was none of the awkwardness that could crop up between couples who'd once tried to be something more.

"Hey." He took a moment to catch his breath. "Are you going to get Thor?"

"Yes. It's so beautiful out, I thought it'd be a nice day to walk."

He placed a hand on her lower back and gestured her forward. "Come on. I'll walk with you for a bit."

"What's going on?" She held her breath, waiting to see if he'd heard the news about Marcia.

"Nothing much, just taking a quick break, but I was wondering if you'd like to go kayaking next Monday?"

Gia stumbled. "Uh..."

Understanding her fear, Trevor grinned. "Come on. It'll be fun."

"Yeah. That's what you said about paddleboarding, and how'd that turn out?"

He full out laughed. "You were doing fine until you freaked out and fell in."

"I freaked out, as you call it, because there was an alligator staring at me."

His eyes went wide. "So falling in seemed like a good idea?"

Gia snorted. It hadn't been her most graceful moment, especially the part where she'd tried to scramble back onto the board and in a moment of blind desperation managed to pull Trevor in with her.

Trevor nudged her with his shoulder. "Besides, he wasn't staring at you. He was just sitting there not paying you any mind at all."

She poked his chest. "You don't know that, mister."

"Okay, okay." He held his hands up in a gesture of surrender. "But kayaking is different."

"Oh yeah? What's different about it?"

"Well, for starters, you're actually inside the kayak, so the alligators can't get you." He swung his head to shift the too long hair out of his eyes, an adorable gesture Gia had grown quite fond of.

"I'll see." She didn't have the heart to tell him she'd decided she wasn't much of an outdoors person.

"Please?"

She groaned. They both knew she was going to give in, just like she'd given in to hiking and paddleboarding. Though, in her defense, she'd held her ground at parasailing. No way was she getting tied to the back of a boat and dragged through the air on a parachute. She shivered at the thought. "Fine. I'll give it a try."

"Yes. You're going to love it. I know it." He took off at a brisk jog before she could change her mind, then tripped going down the curb into the street and waved over his shoulder that he was okay.

Gia laughed. How anyone as clumsy as Trevor could be so athletic when it came to outdoor activities was beyond her, but he was, and he was determined to get her to enjoy at least one of them. She resumed her walk, wondering how in the world she'd gotten roped into joining him yet again. And how she could get out of it before next week.

Chapter 7

Gia checked that all the coffeepots were full, then headed for the front door to open for the day. She could tell before she even unlocked the café door that news of Marcia's murder had spread. Though a few customers occasionally lingered outside waiting for her to open, the current small crowd was unusual. As was the undercurrent buzzing through them. Gossip always offered excitement in Boggy Creek, but this was different. Fear had settled in more than one pair of eyes.

Gia unlocked the door a few minutes early and held it open, greeting everyone with a smile as they entered. Usually, she'd seat each group, but Willow hadn't arrived yet, and she didn't want to keep everyone standing around, so she invited everyone to have a seat wherever they'd like. Most congregated toward the middle of the café or the counter, where they'd be sure not to miss out on any information that got passed around.

Earl tagged along at the back of the line. He tipped the fisherman's cap he always wore on his way past. "Mornin'."

"Good morning, Earl. You're late today." Earl usually knocked on the door half an hour or so before Gia opened, then sat with her and had a cup of coffee until she was ready to unlock the door. She'd begun to look forward to the routine each morning.

"Got a late start, what with all my kids calling me to see what was going on." He winked and headed for his usual spot at the counter.

Gia followed. She grabbed a coffeepot and a stack of menus and weaved her way through the room, filling coffee mugs and making sure everyone had a menu to look at while they waited to place their orders.

Most menus sat closed on the tables while rumors flew.

Esmeralda, an older woman who'd become a regular, stopped Gia on her way by.

"Good morning, Esmeralda. How are you today?"

Esmeralda patted her perfectly coiffed blue hair. Though how she managed to have herself so put together before six o'clock in the morning was beyond her. Gia was lucky to get her mass of dark brown curls shoved into a sloppy knot at the top of her head before running out the door to work in the morning. Maybe Esmeralda slept sitting up.

"Good morning, dear." Esmeralda gestured for her to lean closer and pitched her voice low. As if everyone in the room hadn't already heard about Marcia's unfortunate demise. "Have you heard the news?"

"News?" Gia feigned innocence.

"Yes," Estelle, Esmeralda's twin, looking equally as well composed, chimed in. "Marcia Steers was murdered."

"Oh, yes, I did hear that." She would offer no more than that. Obviously, news of her finding the body hadn't traveled as far as the Bailey twins. At least not yet.

"Can you believe it? There hasn't been a murder in Boggy Creek since… uh…" Estelle's cheeks flamed red and she lowered her head. "Well, it's been a while."

"Yes, it has." Gia pulled an order pad from her apron, giving the woman a chance to collect herself. The first time curiosity had driven Esmeralda and Estelle into the café had been just after Gia's ex-husband, Bradley, was killed. Only that time, they hadn't been convinced of Gia's innocence. She'd since become quite fond of the pair. "What can I get you ladies this morning?"

She jotted down their order, then excused herself and moved on to the next table, leaving Esmeralda to reprimand her sister in private.

She'd taken three orders by the time Willow rushed through the door and looked around the crowded room. She shot Gia a huge grin, grabbed her apron and order pad from behind the counter, and got to work.

Gia ripped the order slips off and tucked her pad into her apron pocket, then turned to head into the kitchen and start cooking. She paused when the front door opened, ready to greet her next customer. Her smile faltered when she came face-to-face with Captain Hayes, but she recovered quickly. "Good morning, Captain."

He nodded.

"Would you like a table, or would you prefer to sit at the counter?"

He studied her a moment, jaw clenched.

She held her ground and his stare. No way she'd allow this man to intimidate her. If he had a problem, he could just get over it. She hadn't done anything wrong, and she was just about over his attitude.

"Counter's fine." He released her gaze and started forward.

Gia followed. She'd seat him and give him a menu, but after that, he was Willow's problem. For the first time she was grateful for having to cook, which allowed her to escape to the kitchen. She realized a moment too late Hayes had stopped, and barely kept from plowing into him. "Captain?"

He ignored her, his attention fully focused on an older man sitting alone at a table toward the back corner.

The man acknowledged him with a slight nod, then went back to perusing his menu.

Hayes only faltered for a moment before resuming his trek toward the counter. He slid onto the stool without ever looking at the other man again. "Just coffee."

She hesitated. She already had three order slips in her hand, and she needed to get them started. Yet, curiosity burned a hole in her gut.

Earl sat only two seats down from Captain Hayes, laughing at something the man next to him said. There was no way to get his attention and ask if he knew the older man without Hayes hearing her.

Dang.

"Willow will be right with you," she told the captain, then strode toward the kitchen with some small sense of satisfaction. Hayes could just wait a few minutes for the coffee he wouldn't bother paying for anyway. Somewhere along the line, he'd gotten the impression whatever he wanted was on the house, even though she'd never once offered to pick up his tab. But it was better to stay off his radar. At least, that's what she'd told herself every time he got up and walked out without so much as looking at the bill she'd left beside his almost empty cup.

Gia tacked her orders above the grill, washed her hands, pulled on a pair of gloves, and tried to shake off the annoyance trying to creep in. Captain Hayes wasn't worth ruining her day over, but she'd be lying if she didn't admit her interest had been piqued by the stranger who'd given him pause.

She sprinkled a handful of diced ham, green peppers, and onions onto the grill to heat, then cracked three eggs into a large bowl, scrambled them, and poured them over the mixture. While the western omelet cooked, she cut a bagel and dropped it into the toaster, then threw a few pieces of sausage and bacon onto the grill. She cut open two rolls, left them open on plates on the counter, cracked four eggs onto the grill, broke the yolks, then flipped the western omelet over and checked the order slips.

Home fries. She spooned two large helpings onto the plates with the rolls, then flipped the eggs over, added cheese to the omelet, and folded it over.

The bagel popped up, so she spread butter on both sides, then slid the omelet onto the plate with the bagel, shoved the plate onto the counter in the cutout between the kitchen and dining room, and took a quick peek.

The man in the back corner still sat nursing his coffee, but Hayes was gone.

Willow rushed in and tacked a small stack of orders above the grill. "Congratulations."

Gia turned. "Huh?"

"You did it."

"Did what?" She put a couple of slices of cheese onto the eggs, then piled them on the rolls with sausage and bacon, added salt and pepper, and put the plates on the counter.

"Gained acceptance. Once you become a gossip hot spot, you're in." Willow gave her a thumbs-up before she grabbed a couple of plates and turned to go.

Gia laughed as warmth rushed through her. She hadn't realized how important acceptance had been to her. Especially when she wasn't even sure she wanted to stay in Boggy Creek. Not for the first time, she wished she could get out from behind the grill and interact, get to know people better, maybe make some friends. It was long past time to hire a cook. "Willow, wait."

She turned back. "What's up?"

"The older gentleman in the back corner... Do you know who he is?"

"No, sorry. Why?"

"Don't worry about it. Just curious. Thanks."

"Yup." She hurried out the door.

Gia returned to filling orders. Several people ordered breakfast pies, which were easy enough, since they were premade and kept beneath warmers. All Gia had to do was cut a piece, add some home fries or grits, and make the toast. She dropped two slices of bread into each of the five toasters lining the countertop, plated two slices of meat lover's pie, two of vegetable pie, and one western. While she waited for the toast to pop up, she ladled pancake batter onto the grill.

The sound of raised voices disrupted her flow.

"She's busy right now." Willow's voice came from right outside the kitchen door. Odd. Gia had never heard her raise her voice before, didn't think she had it in her to be nasty to anyone. Obviously, she'd been wrong. "You can't go back there, Maybelle."

"Oh, really. And who's going to stop me? You?"

Gia spread butter over all ten pieces of toast, cut them, then shifted the plates to the cutout and checked the remaining orders. Too many to stop and deal with Maybelle at the moment, that was for sure.

She flipped the pancakes and scrambled more eggs for omelets, then poured the eggs onto the grill.

Maybelle shoved through the door, then stormed across the kitchen and stopped only two inches away from Gia.

Willow shot Gia an apologetic look. "I'm sorry, Gia, she—"

"Thanks, Willow. Don't worry about it. Everything is fine."

"What did you tell them?" Maybelle demanded.

"Tell whom?" Gia squeezed between Maybelle and the counter and dropped two slices of rye bread into one of the toasters, then plated the pancakes and shifted them to the cutout.

"Don't play games with me, you little twit," she huffed, pointing her finger at Gia. Her cheeks flamed bright red, and a vein throbbed at her temple.

Gia stopped short, for the first time realizing how angry Maybelle was. As much as she disliked the woman, seeing her that distressed tugged at something in her. She resisted the urge to tell her off and call the police to have her forcibly removed. "I'm sorry, Maybelle. I'm completely swamped right now. I don't know what you're so angry with me about, but maybe—"

"Maybe nothing. You know exactly what you did."

Gia nudged past Maybelle to get to the grill before her eggs could burn. The last thing she needed was to burn anything and have to start over. She flipped the omelet over and spooned some of the vegetable mixture onto half of the omelet.

Maybelle's hot breath bathed the back of her neck. "I want to know what you told the police."

"The police?" Had Maybelle heard she'd been the one to find the body? Gia tried to think as she folded the omelet over the vegetables and slid it onto a plate, then buttered the toast and put the plate up for Willow. She turned and started back toward the grill to begin the next order.

Maybelle stood between her and the grill, arms folded across her chest.

"What are you talking about, Maybelle? I don't have time for this." Gia started past her.

Maybelle put a hand against her shoulder, bringing her to an abrupt halt.

Gia eyed her hand, then lifted her gaze to Maybelle and raised a brow.

Although she removed her hand, she made no move to get out of the way. "The police showed up at my house asking questions about Hank and the dead woman, accusing him of having an affair with her."

"Oh...uh..." Uh-oh. Hunt must have turned in the pictures she and Savannah had found. Surely he wouldn't have told anyone they'd been the ones to find them.

"My husband was not fooling around with that woman."

"Okay."

"Excuse me?" Maybelle frowned.

"Look, I'm busy right now, and I really don't understand what any of this has to do with me."

"Don't play innocent with me. I have friends in the department, and I know you were the one to find the body. Now I have cops crawling all over my house because you're trying to implicate me in her murder."

"What! Are you crazy?"

"You told the police that ridiculous lie about my Hank and that woman." She pulled herself straighter and puffed out her chest. "As if he'd ever stray from me."

Gia's mind raced. How would Maybelle know Gia had given Hunt the pictures? Savannah wouldn't have told anyone. And she couldn't imagine Hunt would have. Leo? What reason would he have to say anything? But who else besides the four of them knew?

"Maybelle, I honestly don't know what you're talking about. I never spoke to the police about you at all."

"Oh, really?" She pursed her lips.

"Really." Gia had half a mind to slap the smug look right off her face. So much for the small bit of sympathy that had begun to surface. She tried to count to ten in her head. She only made it to four. "Now, if you'll excuse me, I have work to do. And if you don't leave, I will call the police, and I will have you removed from my café."

"This isn't over, you know. I know you have it in for me. You know what I think?"

She shouldn't encourage her. Knowing that couldn't curb her morbid curiosity. "No. What do you think?"

"I think you're jealous, and that's why you're pointing the finger at me. You couldn't keep your own husband, so now you're hankerin' after mine."

The laugh blurted out an instant before she managed to slap her hand over her mouth to stop it.

"Go ahead and laugh. We're shutting your café down. That's a promise."

Ah jeez. She'd forgotten Maybelle was on the town council.

"What are you going to do then? How are you going to live?" She took another step closer. "Well, let me tell you something, you hussy, you won't be gettin' my husband, no matter what you try to accuse me of."

"Gia?" Willow peeked in the doorway. "Why aren't there any orders up?"

"They're coming now." She sidestepped Maybelle, changed her gloves, and ran her finger over the next order slip in line, trying to bring her focus back to the task at hand. "And do me a favor, Willow. Call the police and have Maybelle removed, please."

Willow's mouth fell open. "Uh…"

"Don't bother." Maybelle waved a hand to dismiss her. "I was just leaving."

Gia's hands shook as she lined bacon onto the grill to heat.

"But don't think this is over."

She only spared Maybelle a quick glance over her shoulder, but it was enough to send a shiver down her spine. For the first time, Gia gave serious consideration to the theory of Maybelle as Marcia Steers's killer.

The cold, calculating look in Maybelle's eyes was all the confirmation she needed to know the woman was up to something. And whatever it was probably didn't bode well for Gia.

Chapter 8

"So, what'd I miss?" Savannah strode through the kitchen doorway, snatched a piece of bacon off the dwindling pile, and popped it in her mouth.

"Sounds like you already heard." Who was she kidding? Savannah probably knew all about Maybelle's visit before the woman had even walked out the door. "Who told you?"

Savannah laughed. "Who didn't?"

"That's about what I figured."

"So, what happened?"

Gia glanced at the clock, stripped off her gloves, and removed her apron. She shoved back a few stray strands of hair that had escaped their knot with her wrist, then washed her hands. "You didn't tell anyone we found those pictures, did you?"

"Of course not. You think I want to earn Hunt's wrath?"

No. She wouldn't. Especially after they'd gotten off so easy after going—breaking, whatever—into Marcia's house. "Would Hunt or Leo have told anyone?"

"I doubt it. Besides, if they had, we'd more than likely be having this conversation with Captain Hayes down at the station."

"True." Hayes would be in his glory, gloating with the two of them at his mercy. "So how did Maybelle know?"

"About the pictures?"

"I don't know. She didn't actually mention the pictures. She said I accused Hank of having an affair with Marcia. Said I was jealous and wanted him for myself."

Savannah didn't even try to stifle her laugher. "You have got to be kidding me."

"Nope. I wish I was." She started wrapping the trays of bacon and sausage she had cooked—once the all-day rush had finally slowed—in preparation for the next morning.

"Well, don't worry about her." Savannah started washing the dishes Gia hadn't gotten to earlier.

"Yeah, well, she threatened again to shut the café down. Just what I need, an enemy on the council." Gia sighed as she slid a tray into the refrigerator.

"I told you, don't worry about her. Everyone knows that one's nuttier than a squirrel turd. No one's gonna pay her any mind."

Gia tried to shrug the encounter off, but it wasn't so easy now that she wasn't hustling to get orders out. "What are you doing here, anyway? I thought you were showing a house tonight."

"Client canceled." She finished the last dish, turned off the water, and dried her hands, then hooked an arm through Gia's. "So I figured we'd go out to dinner. We haven't had a girls' night since... Actually, I can't remember the last time we had a girls' night."

"I'm sorry, Savannah. I can't. I have to pick Thor up from day care."

"Already taken care of. Joey's picking him up and taking him to my house. He'll take care of him until we get home." She smiled and nudged Gia with her shoulder. "Come on. It'll be fun. You need to relax a little."

"You know what?" She'd fallen into the habit of going straight home after work every day. If she was going to live in Florida, it was time to start getting out and doing more. Maybe she'd find it more enjoyable if she got out and had a little fun now and then. What did she really have to rush home to, anyway? "That sounds great."

Savannah's eyes lit up. "Awesome."

"Where do you want to go?"

"Let's just get done and get out of here." She started putting the dishes away. "Our reservations are for eight."

Gia didn't bother to ask where they were going. Past experience had taught her Savannah could be surprisingly tight-lipped when she wanted to be. As she had been about her mother's death for a long time. Although Savannah had told Gia her mother passed away, it had been years after they'd met that Gia had found out any of the details relating to Sara Mills's murder. "Did you recognize any of the other names on the list?"

Savannah's posture stiffened. "I'm not sure."

"What do you mean?' Gia dropped another bag onto the pile by the back door. Taking the garbage out to the dumpster still brought a small jolt of apprehension. She shook it off and returned to cleaning up.

"The bar that used to be here? It was called McNeil's."

"You think the Sean McNeil on the list was the owner?"

"I don't know. I guess he could have been." Savannah poured the last of the coffee from the pot down the sink.

Wiping down the counter, Gia looked around and resigned herself to the fact that everything else was done. She was going to have to take the garbage out if she ever wanted to get out of there. "What ever happened to him?"

Savannah washed out the pot. "No idea."

Gia had procrastinated as long as possible. She unlocked the back door, gathered the bags in her hands, and shoved the door open with her hip.

The short walk across the parking lot seemed to take forever, her mind conjuring an image of Bradley's arm hanging out of the dumpster before she could stop it. She used her arm to wipe the sweat from her brow, cursing Bradley for bringing so much pain to her life, then tamped down the guilt that immediately followed any negative thoughts about her ex.

She tried to refocus her thoughts. What could Sara Mills have wanted with information about the café? Well, bar then. Maybe. And did it have anything to do with her death?

She shifted the bags to free up a hand, pushed the dumpster lid open, dropped the bags in, turned, and hurried back across the lot.

Savannah stood in the doorway, holding the door open. Sympathy shone in her eyes.

"Thanks," Gia said as she rushed through the door, pulled it shut, and turned the key in the lock. She hurried to the sink to wash her hands.

Savannah held out a paper towel. "You okay?"

"I will be." She took the paper towel and dried her hands, then laid a hand on Savannah's arm. "Thanks."

"Sure thing. It gets easier, you know."

"What does?"

"Living with the pain of losing someone. And the guilt." She patted Gia's hand, where it still rested on her arm, then offered a small smile. "Come on. Time to eat."

Gia accepted the change of subject, though she couldn't miss the hurt Savannah tried so hard to hide. She quickly locked up and followed Savannah to her car. While Savannah drove, Gia's mind wandered back to the list. At least two of the five people on the list were dead. Both murdered. Captain Hayes was still alive, but he'd signed out the same folder only days after Sara Mills was killed. Now he was in charge of the investigation into Marcia's death. But only after he'd thrown Hunt off the case.

And what about the other names on the list? Sean McNeil and Floyd Masters? Where were they? Was it possible one of them was the killer? Or maybe the next victim? Researching both of their names shot to the top of her to-do list. As soon as she got home and settled Thor, she'd type their names into Google and see what she could find out.

"What do you think?" Savannah pulled into a small lakefront parking lot.

Gia looked around, but nothing seemed familiar, and she'd been too lost in her own thoughts while Savannah drove to keep track of her surroundings. "Where are we?"

"Lakeshore Pier. The best seafood place around." She got out and waited for Gia, then started toward what looked like a houseboat. "Beautiful, isn't it?"

Though it was already dark, there was enough light to make out the silhouette of the woods surrounding the large lake. Scattered lights dotted the woods where an occasional house sat amid the forest. Moonlight rippled across the lake's surface. "Gorgeous."

Soft lighting ran along the base of the pier, lining both sides, the reflections shimmering against the lake's dark water. A two-story structure with a wraparound porch sat at the end of the long pier. A few people sat on wicker chairs with drinks in their hands, trays of appetizers sitting on low tables in the center of each seating arrangement.

Gia's stomach growled. "Do you think the wait will be long?"

"We won't have to wait at all." Savannah stepped up to a podium and gave the hostess her name.

"Right this way, please." The hostess walked across the restaurant and up a flight of stairs in the back corner. She emerged on a terrace that took up the whole roof.

From where they stood Gia had an unobstructed view of the entire lake. The darkness did nothing to diminish its beauty. If anything, Gia thought it probably added to the allure.

Palm trees swayed in the slight breeze as the hostess led them to a small wrought iron table beside the railing. She left them to peruse their menus with a promise the waitress would be with them shortly.

Gia left her menu sitting on the table and stared out across the lake. "This really is amazing, Savannah."

"Just wait until you taste the food."

"I can't wait." She dragged her gaze from the serenity the view offered and opened her menu. "What's good?"

"I usually have the steak and lobster tails."

"Is the steak tender?"

"Melts in your mouth." Savannah closed her menu and dropped it onto the table.

Gia followed. "Steak and lobster tails it is then."

The waitress arrived and took their orders, then disappeared with the menus.

Savannah stared out over the lake, her lower lip caught between her teeth. A sure sign something was bothering her.

Gia stayed quiet.

Savannah would talk in her own time and her own way.

Until then, Gia enjoyed the peaceful evening. She certainly couldn't complain about the Florida weather in the winter. While New York was buried under a foot of snow, Florida boasted temperatures in the sixties with a soft breeze.

The waitress arrived with their drinks and set them on bamboo coasters.

Gia stirred her virgin piña colada, then took a sip. "Wow. Now this is the vision I had of what Florida living would be like."

Savannah laughed, but it did nothing to disguise the hurt in her eyes. "Does that mean it goes in the plus column?"

Though the comment had been made in jest, the underlying pain in Savannah's voice was undeniable. Maybe it was time to just be honest.

"It's been a hard adjustment, moving down here."

"I know. I remember when I moved to New York." She sipped her drink. "I never did get used to living there."

Gia didn't know what to say. She'd never lie to Savannah, but she honestly didn't know what the truth was. She had no idea if she'd stay in Florida forever.

"I'd understand if you decide to move back, you know?"

"I know you would." Of that much she was certain. Savannah would stand by her side no matter what. Which would make hurting her all the more difficult. Gia forced a smile. "But tonight definitely goes in the plus column."

This time, Savannah's smile was genuine. She held up her glass. "To tonight, then."

Gia clinked her glass against Savannah's. "It's not that I don't like Florida. It's just different. So different. And sometimes I get homesick."

"Believe me, as much as I don't want to, I understand. That's why I brought it up. I want you to know it's okay if you move back." She set her glass aside and sulked. "Heck, if they close the café down, I can't even say I'd blame you."

Gia's heart ached. She couldn't deny her thoughts had pretty much followed the same track Savannah's had, but she also couldn't take seeing Savannah so disappointed. "Let's not get ahead of ourselves. I'm not going anywhere yet, and I have no intention of letting anyone shut me down without putting up a fight."

Savannah looked into her eyes, searching for something, her lime green fingernails tapping a steady rhythm against the tabletop.

Gia laid a hand on top of hers. "If I leave, Savannah, it will be because it's the best choice for me, not because someone chased me away."

"Good. Because as much as I love having you here, I wouldn't want you to stay if it didn't make you happy."

Gia sat back. Something was bothering Savannah, of that she was certain. She didn't doubt Savannah loved her and wanted her to stay close, but she'd never been needy, had always wanted Gia to be happy. Even when she'd known marrying Bradley was a mistake, she'd backed off and allowed Gia to figure it out on her own. Why now, all of a sudden, was it so important to her that Gia stay?

Gia shook off the thought. No matter what happened, as long as Savannah needed her, she wasn't going anywhere.

Savannah twirled her glass in the ring of condensation on her coaster, staring deep into the swirling contents. "So…"

Gia waited.

A blush crept up Savannah's cheeks. "Leo asked me to marry him. Again."

"And? Did you say yes?" Savannah hadn't told Gia about Leo's numerous marriage proposals; Hunt had.

"No." She looked up from beneath her lashes. "But at least this time I didn't say no."

"What did you say?"

She sighed and sat back. "I told him to give me a little time to think about it."

Leo must have been in his glory. He'd been waiting years for Savannah to say yes. At least now she was one step closer.

"Do you love him?"

"Yes. With all my heart. You know, there was a time I even considered not going to New York to stay and marry him."

"I could understand not wanting to give up your dreams, and Leo is an amazing man for putting your happiness ahead of his own, and then waiting for you to figure out what you need. But I don't understand what's holding you back now?"

She frowned. "My dad."

"He doesn't like Leo?"

"Oh no, quite the opposite, he loves Leo, thinks he'd be great for me." She laughed. "And he wants more grandchildren."

Yikes. Gia hadn't considered Savannah might get married and have children right away. The thought of children seemed such a far-off idea for Gia.

"And we already know Hunt wants me to marry him, since he threatened to beat him senseless if he didn't propose before I left for New York."

Gia couldn't help laughing. Hunt had told her that, but she hadn't realized Savannah knew about it. "How'd you find out?"

"Oh, please. This is Boggy Creek. That incident kept the rumor mill churning for weeks."

The waitress set their appetizers in the center of the table. "Can I get you ladies anything else?"

"Not right now, thank you," Gia said, hoping Savannah would continue to confide in her despite the interruption.

The waitress smiled and left.

Savannah spooned a few melon balls onto her plate, and Gia was afraid it signaled the end of their conversation.

"So what does your dad have to do with you saying no to Leo?"

She speared a melon ball with her fork, then laid the fork on her plate without taking a bite and folded her hands on the table. "How long have you known me?"

"More than ten years."

"And of those ten years, you've been my best friend for almost all of them."

"Yes." She and Savannah had taken an instant liking to each other, becoming roommates almost immediately after they met and living together for almost five years. Never mind best friends, they were sisters.

"And in that time, how many times have you seen my father?"

Gia couldn't really remember. "Not more than a handful."

"My mom and dad were married very young, right out of high school. Heck, they were already engaged when they graduated. They had my brother ten months later."

She inhaled a shaky breath before continuing. "When my mother was killed, my dad fell into a depression. He used to be a friendly, outgoing man. Now... Well, now he barely leaves the house, just stays cooped up with his dogs, lost in memories of a time when he shared his life with the only woman he ever loved."

Savannah looked up and stared Gia right in the eyes. "Leo is a cop, Gia. Granted, he's a cop in Boggy Creek, but still… Bad things happen everywhere. Even here."

"Oh, Savannah. I'm so sorry about your dad, but—"

"I don't know if I can live like that, waiting every night for him to come home, never knowing for certain that he will." A tear rolled down her cheek, and she swiped it away with her napkin. "I love him. With all my heart. I have since we were kids, but after watching my mother's death destroy a man I always thought of as a rock, I don't know if I can handle being with him."

Gia resisted the urge to reach out to Savannah while she struggled to regain her composure. Her hold on her emotions seemed so fragile that Gia didn't want to do anything that would make her lose control. "Savannah, there's no guarantee that anyone will come home at the end of any given day. I understand it's much different when your spouse does something dangerous for a living, but in the end, isn't it better to have shared your life with the person you loved, no matter what? Do you think your father regrets the years he was fortunate enough to spend with your mother?"

Savannah sort of smiled through her tears and shook her head.

Gia lowered her voice even more. "Besides, your father's circumstances were a little different. It wasn't only losing your mother he had to deal with."

"No…" She sniffled. "It wasn't. He also had to endure the suspicion cast on him by Captain Hayes. A man who should have been working to find out who really killed my mother." Her jaw clenched as anger replaced some of the sadness.

"Have you talked to Leo about how you feel?"

"No. Leo has wanted to be a cop since we were little kids. His father was a cop. His brother is a cop. He's never wanted to do anything else." She inhaled deeply, finally gaining control, and met Gia's gaze. "There's nothing Leo wouldn't do for me, and I'm terrified he'd give up his dream to be with me. When I wanted to go to New York to be a dancer, Leo sat and waited for me for five years. When I came back, he still waited. He loves me more than life, the way my father loves my mother. And that scares me to death too."

The waitress arrived with their salads. She frowned at the uneaten appetizers. "Would you like me to take those?"

"No, thanks. We're still working on them." Savannah smiled. Though her eyes remained a bit red-rimmed from crying, no other outward sign of her sadness remained.

Gia had no doubt their conversation had just ended.

The waitress placed their salads in front of them and asked if they wanted anything else.

Savannah ordered water with lemon for both of them.

Gia's attention wandered across the terrace to the dark silhouette of the woods surrounding the lake. So beautiful, and yet a little scary knowing she lived smack in the middle of woods like that. Dark. Dangerous. Teeming with life.

For the first time since Bradley's killer had been apprehended, a chill crept up her spine, and the feeling of being watched overwhelmed her.

"You okay, Gia?" Savannah frowned. "You looked a million miles away there for a minute."

She tried to shake off her unease. Maybe all Savannah's talk about her mother had spooked her. "Yeah. Sorry, my mind just wandered."

"No problem, now dig in. These melon balls are amazing." Savannah popped one into her mouth and closed her eyes. "Mmm…"

Gia took a bite, but she barely tasted it as her gaze fell on a man seated alone at the far corner of the terrace. Though he remained shrouded in shadow, Gia was almost positive it was the same older man who'd been seated in the café earlier. The same man who'd made Captain Hayes pause.

He seemed to be staring into his water glass as he ran a finger around its rim.

She glanced away quickly, hoping he didn't notice her looking at him, and leaned toward Savannah. "Don't turn around yet, but when I start eating, look over your shoulder to the far corner of the terrace and see if you know the man sitting there."

Gia sat up straighter, willing her gaze to remain on her salad, and took a bite.

Savannah waited a moment, then looked around as if searching for the waitress. "What man?"

When Gia looked up, he was gone.

Chapter 9

Gia hooked Thor's leash over her wrist and got out of the car, bear spray in one hand, keys in the other. She wasn't sure she'd ever get used to coming home to the darkness of the woods surrounding her small house, and the chill she'd gotten earlier at the restaurant had never fully disappeared.

She searched the shadows among the trees, while trying to keep an eye on the ground in front of her in case a snake decided to take a nap on her walkway. It was long past time to go through the junk she still had left in the garage from the move and get rid of it. If she hadn't missed it by now, she probably didn't need it. Maybe she'd just get a dumpster and toss it all in the trash. At least then she could pull into the garage.

Thankful she'd put the porch light on a timer, she turned the key in the lock, shoved the door open, and ushered Thor through as fast as she could. Once she slammed the door behind her and locked it, she took a deep breath.

Thor sat staring at her, used to the crazy routine of getting in the house, and waited for her to take his leash off.

"Good boy, Thor." She petted his head and unhooked the leash from his collar. "Let's get you out and ready for bed."

It was much later than she usually came home, and she had to get up early in the morning to make it to the café in time to do some of the prep work she'd neglected in order to go out with Savannah. It was worth it, though. Despite the serious conversation that had started the night, they'd enjoyed themselves throughout dinner. It was nice to relax with a friend for a change.

She turned on every light as she strode through the living room to the kitchen. She turned on the back deck light and checked for wildlife, or anything else that might be lurking in the shadows, before opening the door and letting Thor out.

on the nightstand, and she longed to pick it up and lose herself in the story for a little while, but it was too late for that too. She needed to sleep, at least for a few hours.

If Thor would just stop pacing in front of the door.

"Thor, lie down."

He studied the closed door once more, then ignored his crate and lay across the doorway, sulking.

"He'll be fine, Thor. Right now he just needs to be alone." Gia lay down, closed her eyes, and allowed herself to drift. She'd expected to fall asleep the instant her head hit the pillow, but it didn't seem that was going to happen. She cracked her eyes open and glanced at the nightstand clock just in time to see it creep a minute closer to her alarm going off.

She groaned.

Exhaustion burned her eyes and she let them fall shut again. She dozed in and out, fitfully. Too much on her mind to allow a peaceful rest.

What reason could anyone have had to kill Marcia? Maybelle was the only person she could think of who had any kind of motive.

Bradley had cheated on Gia, numerous times, but no matter how angry or hurt or upset Gia had been, she'd never once even thought about killing him, and yet, people killed in fits of jealous rage all the time.

Which brought her back to Hunt. Savannah thought he already knew about Marcia and Hank, but when had he found out? And how would he have reacted when he did? She had no idea, but she did know he wouldn't have killed her.

But maybe Hank had. He'd have had the opportunity. It wouldn't have been hard to lure his lover out to the woods and kill her. But why?

Thor lurched to his feet and started barking. He scratched at the door.

Gia threw back the blanket and jumped out of bed. "What's the matter, boy?"

She'd never seen him like this, like he was frantic to get out of the room. She'd left her bear spray in her purse in the kitchen. Though she hated guns, she kept a baseball bat in the garage. First thing in the morning, she'd grab it and put it under her bed. Of course, that did nothing to help her current situation.

She yanked her jeans on over her boxer shorts, threw a shirt over her pajama tank, and jammed her feet into her sneakers without bothering with socks. She didn't want Thor to run out into the unknown, but she didn't have his leash in the bedroom, so she had to settle for holding his collar. "Stay, boy."

She flung open the door, and the smell of smoke hit her in the face.

Chapter 10

"Hunt?" Gia released Thor's collar and ran down the hallway.

Thor remained glued to her side.

"Hunt!" The smell of smoke got stronger as she ran. Hunt's bed was made up on the couch, but there was no sign of him in the living room, nor in the kitchen. The thin blanket she'd left for him lay crumpled on the floor. "Hunt, where are you?"

The fire alarm started blaring.

Thor barked again. This time, he didn't stop.

She recalled the signs she'd seen all over the county, warning of the dry conditions, the risk of the entire neighborhood going up in flames.

Okay, think, Gia. Think. She couldn't through Thor's frantic barking.

"It's okay, Thor." She patted his head, offering what reassurance she could in her current state. She had to find Hunt. The memory of his injuries worried her. Had someone found him and decided to finish the job? She ran back to her bedroom, grabbed the phone, and dialed 911.

"911. What is your emergency?"

Gia gave her address and then said, "I smell smoke and my fire alarm is going off."

"Do you see smoke or flames?"

"No. I've walked through the whole house, but I didn't go outside, and I was just about to check the garage."

"Okay, go ahead and check the garage, but feel if the door is hot before you open it."

She pressed a hand against the door. It didn't feel hot, so she cracked it open. Smoke filtered in through the open door, and flames spiked high just outside the window. She slammed the door shut, frantic to find Hunt.

He must have gone outside. "The garage is filled with smoke and I can see flames through the window!"

"Shut the door."

"I did."

"Is anyone else in the house with you?"

"Detective Hunter Quinn was here. He was hurt, and now I can't find him," she blurted. "I have to go check outside."

"No. Stay where you are. Wet towels and put them against the crack beneath the door."

"I can't. I have to find—"

"You have to stay put until we know what's happening there. Going outside might be more dangerous."

"Okay." She started to turn and tripped over Thor, landing hard on her knee. "Sorry, boy."

Thor scrambled backward.

She jumped to her feet and limped to the linen closet.

"I've already dispatched help. They should be there shortly."

"Okay, thank you." With nothing more to say, she settled for thanking the woman again and hung up. She dialed Hunt's number. His cell phone vibrated against the living room coffee table. She disconnected and looked out the front windows.

The fire's glow lit the night, but she couldn't see flames. Nor could she see Hunt. She ran to the back door. Nothing.

Thor still barked frantically.

Indecision beat at her. She had to find Hunt, but she couldn't take Thor outside. The smoke couldn't be good for him. And she wouldn't put him in danger. Yet, she couldn't crate him. What if something happened to her and she couldn't get back to him and the house went up in flames? A wave of nausea hit her. She pulled a dish towel from a drawer, soaked it in water from the sink, and started toward the living room.

Thor followed at her heel.

"Thor, stay."

He whined but continued to pace the small kitchen.

Gia ran through the living room. She looked out the window and pressed her hand against the cool surface before cracking the door open, slipping through, and shutting the door behind her. Flames engulfed the wooded area between her house and the one next door. They licked at the side of the garage.

"Hunt!"

No sign of him.

"Hunt?"

Men's raised voices came from the side of the house. She couldn't tell how many but definitely more than one.

Gia ran toward the road, then cut across the driveway toward the far side of the garage, keeping a good distance between her and the flames… and whatever else might be waiting in the dark. She pressed the towel against her nose and mouth.

A man and a teenage boy with something slung over his shoulder ran up the road toward her. The man yelled, "Do you have another spigot?"

"Uh…" Gia had no idea what was going on.

"We're using both." Hunt emerged from the side of the house, hose in hand, stream directed at the wall of flames beside her garage.

Relief rushed through her.

A man she didn't know, dressed in plaid pajama pants, a tank top, and slippers rounded the garage from behind Hunt. He pointed toward the house next door, on the other side of the burning trees and yelled, "Use mine, Jim, and get it from the other side."

Jim nodded and gestured for the boy to cut across her neighbor's yard. He grabbed one end of the long hose the boy had over his shoulder.

The boy unrolled the hose as he ran toward the house, presumably to attach it to her neighbor's spigot.

The man in the pajamas pointed at Hunt. "We're probably gonna lose the garage. We've gotta soak the roof."

"Got it, Scott." Hunt yanked the hose Gia could now see was hooked up to the spigot at the front of her house and backed away from the flames. He redirected the flow of water toward the roof.

Sirens—a lot of sirens—blared through the night, drowning out the crackle of the flames.

Thor! Gia ran back up the front yard toward the house.

"Get Thor," Hunt yelled.

"I'm going." She burst through the front door, tossed the dish towel aside, and grabbed one of Thor's leashes from a basket in the foyer.

Thor jumped up, planting his front paws against her chest.

She gave him a quick hug, then hooked the leash to his collar. Should she try to salvage anything else? With Thor safely leashed at her side, she ran toward the kitchen and grabbed her purse and stuffed her cell phone inside it. "Come on, boy."

Gia ran back out and joined a group of neighbors who'd gathered by the road in front of her house.

"What happened?" An older woman pulled her bathrobe tighter around her.

"I don't know. My dog started barking, so I got up to see what was going on and smelled smoke."

"Seems to have started in the woods next to the house," she observed as she petted Thor's head. "You're a good boy waking your mama."

Thor looked back and forth between Gia and the woman.

"That's odd. There's nothing over there that could have ignited it." Gia racked her brain but couldn't think of anything that would have started the blaze. "Lightning?"

Maybe she'd fallen into a deeper sleep than she realized and hadn't noticed a storm. They seemed to flare up out of nowhere in Florida.

"Not that I heard, but you never do know."

The first fire truck pulled up, the chaos of the firefighters clambering out of the truck and unwinding hoses making it impossible to hear the woman if she said anything else.

Thor bounced back and forth from one side to the other.

A squad car skidded to a stop, and Leo jumped out. He ran to Gia. "Are you and Thor all right?"

She nodded.

"Where's Hunt?"

"Over there." She gestured toward where she'd last seen him, but she'd lost sight of him in the confusion of the firefighters arriving.

"How badly is he hurt?" Leo started in the direction she'd indicated.

She hurried beside him. "Hurt?"

"The call came over as an officer down. When I recognized the address, I figured it was Hunt."

"Oh, uh…" Uh-oh. She hadn't realized it would sound that way when she'd spoken to the 911 operator. "Sorry. I didn't mean to make it sound like that. He's okay. It's just…"

Leo took her elbow and indicated a fire hose on the ground a few feet in front of them.

She stepped over the hose and watched to make sure Thor didn't trip. She didn't know how much Hunt would want anyone to know, but as soon as Leo laid eyes on him he'd know there'd been a fight. "He showed up on my doorstep a few hours ago. He didn't tell me what happened, but he had a black eye and a split lip. If the condition of his knuckles was any indication, it should be pretty easy to tell if you find whomever he fought with."

"All right." Leo swiped a hand over his mouth, glancing back and forth between Gia and the fire. "Go back and wait with the others. I'll find him and see what's going on."

Gia nodded and turned. No matter how much she wanted to know what was happening, saving her house and probably every other house in the neighborhood, which was pretty much a tinderbox at the moment, took priority.

Leo yelled after her. "And if you know what's good for you, call Savannah and let her know what's going on before she hears your house is on fire and Hunt is hurt."

Yikes. She hadn't thought about how that sounded, but Hunt's family would be worried sick once that rumor reached them. She returned to the street, but instead of joining the growing group of onlookers, she led Thor to a somewhat quiet spot across the street, took her phone out of her purse, and dialed Savannah.

Her groggy voice came over the line after four rings. "Gia? Is something wrong?"

"Everyone is okay, but I wanted to call you before the gossip mill started running for the day." She shot Leo a silent thank-you for reminding her to call. "There's a fire in the woods by my house. It seems to have spread to the garage, but the firefighters are here, and Hunt and some of my neighbors were trying to fight it until they arrived."

The rustle of sheets came over the line, and she figured Savannah was getting out of bed, probably getting ready to rush right over.

"What was Hunt doing there?" Savannah's voice was already strained, even without knowing about the fight. "I was trying to reach him all night, and he never called me ba—oh, uh... Fireworks set the woods on fire?"

Gia laughed wearily. "No, silly. It wasn't like that."

"Oh, well, sorry to hear it."

Leave it to Savannah to worry about her love life while the forest burned down around her.

"So, what was he doing there?"

How much to tell her? Not like she wasn't going to find out. "He stopped by earlier. He'd gotten in a fight and showed up on my doorstep."

"Was he hurt? Hold on." She moved the phone away from her ear, but Gia could still hear her as she woke Joey and told him to get dressed. "All right. I'm back."

"You don't have to come all the way out here, Savannah, though I do appreciate it. Everyone is okay."

Hunt and Leo raced toward her. Savannah said something, but Gia missed what it was as Hunt and Leo jumped into Leo's patrol car and peeled out, then rocketed down the street.

"Gia? Gia!"

"Oh, uh, sorry, Savannah. Leo and Hunt just took off in an awful hurry."

"Do you know where they were headed?"

"No idea."

"I asked who he got into a fight with."

"I have no idea. He wouldn't tell me."

"Okay, hang up and stay where you are. Joey and I are on our way."

Gia disconnected and dropped her phone into her bag. No sense arguing with Savannah. Once she got something in her mind, there was no swaying her. She petted Thor.

Now what? She stood and watched the firefighters. The flames seemed to have diminished considerably. Hopefully, they'd get it under control before it got out of hand.

"Do you know how it started?" A young woman stood beside her with a toddler on her hip.

"I don't know. I woke up to my dog barking like crazy."

"Lucky thing."

Gia weaved her fingers through Thor's thick fur. "Yeah."

"This whole neighborhood could have gone up with how dry it's been lately." Her tone held a note of accusation. As if Gia had done something either stupid or intentional to cause the fire. "You're new here."

She bristled but refrained from telling her off. "Yes, I am, but I'm well aware of fire safety, and I'm quite sure I didn't do anything to cause the fire."

"I hope not." The woman sauntered away, clutching her child a little tighter.

Gia sighed. How could she blame the woman? Most of her neighbors probably felt the same way. In the few months she'd lived in Boggy Creek she'd been connected to one dead body and one forest fire in their community. Although, to be fair, no one had outright said she'd caused the fire. Just because it had started beside her house didn't mean it was her fault. Of course, technically, neither was the dead body.

The fire did bring to light one disturbing fact. She had no clue if there were any fire roads or back exits that led out of the development. She'd only ever come in and out through the front entrance. She'd have to ask around. If there were no fire roads, maybe she could get the board of directors to establish some, even if they were nothing more than dirt trails.

blood, along with two swollen, black eyes, was interfering with his vision, so he called Maybelle to pick him up. They had an argument, though she was stingy on the details, and he mumbled something about someone getting what he deserved and took off on foot."

"Will he come after you?"

Hunt started to laugh, then winced and touched his lip. "I doubt Hank wants another go at me anytime soon."

Under the circumstances, Gia probably would have done the same thing Maybelle claimed she'd done. She'd have gotten into the car and driven past anywhere she might expect to find her husband. Anywhere the target of his anger was known to hang out. "Do you believe her?"

"Hell, I have no idea. I don't know what to believe anymore." He shoved his chair back, stood, and started to pace.

"Where is she now?" The last thing Gia needed was a repeat of Maybelle's appearance at the café.

"She called a friend to come pick her up."

"Who?" From what Gia had heard, Maybelle didn't have too many friends.

"Some guy named Floyd Masters."

"Floyd Masters?" Why did she know that name?

"I don't know who he is, but apparently he sits on the council with her."

That's it. The list. His name was on the list of people who'd signed out the folder with the café paperwork. She'd planned on Googling his name when she'd gotten home earlier, but she'd forgotten all about it.

Hunt stopped pacing in front of the door and pressed the heels of his hands against his eyes. "All I know is a woman who trusted me came to me for help…"

He gripped the doorknob. "And I failed her."

She wanted desperately to alleviate the pain and guilt he was suffering. She stood and laid a hand on his shoulder. "Hunt, you can't torment yourself—"

"You can go, Gia. Thank you for coming in." He jerked the door open, then froze.

"What are you doing here?" A vein throbbed at the side of Captain Hayes's temple, his face beet red, bordering on purple.

Hunt glanced over his shoulder at Gia. "Talking to a friend."

"What's *she* doing here?"

Hunt shrugged. "I have no idea. Hanging out, I guess."

Captain Hayes drilled a finger into Hunt's chest. "I already warned you once. You are off this case." Spittle sprayed from the captain's mouth, and he stepped back and pointed toward the door. "As of now, you are suspended. Leave your shield and your weapon and get the hell out of here."

Hunt glared at him. His hand shook when he pulled his shield from his pocket and threw it at the captain. It hit him smack in the middle of his chest, then dropped onto the floor.

Hayes lowered his voice. "That's it. You have exactly ten seconds to get out of here before I take you into custody."

Hunt stared at his captain for another moment, then stormed out. The door slammed shut behind him, and Gia jumped.

Thor barked once and looked up at her.

She petted his head. A bead of sweat dripped down the side of her face as she stared at the door, waiting for Captain Hayes to come back in and demand answers from her about why she was there.

Hunt had told her to leave. And she was desperate to follow his advice. But where was she supposed to go? And how was she supposed to get there? Her car was back at the house, blocked in the driveway by a gazillion fire trucks.

Her mind whirled through excuses for her presence that Captain Hayes would believe and wouldn't get Hunt in any more trouble than he was already in.

Savannah poked her head in. "Okay if I come in?"

Relief rushed through her. "Sure."

Savannah went straight for Gia and threw her arms around her. "I'm glad you're okay."

Gia hugged her back, then flopped into her chair. "I'm sorry. I should have called and told you I was leaving."

She waved off the apology and sat beside her, stopping first to pet Thor. "No worries, Leo called and told me, so Joey and I came right here. Do you have a lot of damage?"

"I don't even know. It didn't seem like it would be too bad. The firefighters were getting it under control when I left. The only things I saw burning were the patch of woods between my neighbor's house and my house, and the side of the garage."

Savannah squeezed her hand, then pulled her to her feet. "Do you have any idea how lucky you are?"

"Yeah, I do." Gia looked around the empty room. "Where's Joey?"

"He went to see Hunt, but as soon as he's done, we'll give you a ride home."

"Did you see Hunt on the way in?"

"No, why?"

"He just left here."

Savannah frowned. "Was he okay?"

"I'm not sure. Hayes suspended him."

Savannah pursed her lips but didn't seem as surprised as Gia would have expected.

"You don't have anything to say?"

"What can I say? Hayes is an ass." She hooked her arm through Gia's. "Now, come on. Let's get you home."

Gia made no move to leave.

Savannah widened her eyes and stared pointedly at Gia. "Joey will take care of Hunt. Now be quiet and let's go."

Gia looked around what was probably an interrogation room. She should have realized there could be cameras hidden somewhere. Which meant Captain Hayes could know exactly why Hunt had been there. She let the matter drop. "There's no sense in going home. I have to get the café open. As it is I'm going to be late."

"Well, you can't go in looking like that."

Gia hadn't given any thought to her appearance. She looked down at the wrinkled clothes she'd thrown on over her pajamas. She couldn't even imagine what her hair and makeup looked like.

"And you need a shower before you go anywhere." Savannah pinched her nose closed. "You stink like smoke."

She should have realized that sooner, since she smelled it on everyone else.

Savannah tugged her toward the door. "Come on."

"Where are we going?"

"My house. You can shower, and I'll lend you something to wear. I have a few longer skirts that might work." She grinned. "Though they'll be a lot shorter on you."

Gia smiled. Leave it to Savannah to take care of everything. Savannah, like Hunt, was the kind of friend you could always depend on. "Savannah?"

"Yup?" She took Thor's leash from the table and clipped it to his collar, then led him from the room.

Gia walked beside her, keeping her voice low. "Do you remember the list of names we found earlier?"

"Yes." Her voice wavered, barely noticeable as they walked down the hallway, but Gia knew her too well to miss it.

"Do you remember the name Floyd Masters?"

"Of course. You asked about him earlier. Why?"

"Because Hunt said he picked Maybelle up from the station a little while ago."

"The station? What was Maybelle doing here?" Savannah pushed through a set of double doors, then held one open for Gia.

Several officers looked their way as they crossed a large, open room filled with desks. Gia lowered her voice even more. "Didn't Leo tell you what was going on?"

"No, he didn't have time. Why? What's Maybelle got to do with anything?"

"I'll fill you in on the way to your house, but Hunt said Masters sits on the council with Maybelle."

Savannah handed Gia Thor's leash, pulled out her phone, dialed, and pressed the phone against her ear.

"Who are you calling?"

"Tommy."

"But it's the middle of the night!"

"Hunt was hurt." And that was all the explanation needed. One of their own had been hurt, so the whole family would sit up all night awaiting word. Savannah shifted the phone and said, "Hey, Tommy. He's okay. Joey went to find him, but I spoke to Leo, and he's okay. I wanted to ask you something, though. What do you know about Floyd Masters?"

Gia held the front door open for Savannah, then followed her out into the morning chill. Even though it was cooler overnight, the humidity still made the air feel thick. It also burned her eyes. Or maybe that was the smoke remnants clinging to her clothes and hair. Or it could be exhaustion. Probably all the above.

She hooked the leash over her wrist and rubbed her eyes as they started toward the car. She had no idea how she was going to get through the day on zero sleep, but she didn't have a choice.

Savannah hit the button to unlock the car, then stopped beside it. "Yeah... uh huh... Do you know if he's friends with Maybelle?"

Tommy's voice mumbled over the line, but it was too muffled for Gia to make out what he was saying.

Savannah's eyes widened. "Are you sure?"

He issued a short reply.

"Okay, thanks, Tommy. Yes. I will. Good night." She disconnected the call and stared at Gia across the roof of the car. "Masters does sit on the council, but Tommy doesn't know him well. Says he mostly stays to himself."

"Is he friends with Maybelle?"

"Not that Tommy knew of, but he did know someone he's related to, thinks he's the guy's uncle or something like that."

"Who?"

Savannah looked around the fairly deserted parking lot and lowered her voice. "None other than our good friend, Captain Howard Hayes."

Chapter 12

Gia hopped out of Savannah's car, thanked her for the ride, and the shower, and the clothes, and everything else, and hurried up the walkway, key in hand, to the café. She unlocked the door, went in and closed it behind her, then locked it again, leaving the key dangling from the lock. Earl would be there shortly, and she'd have to open it again anyway.

She strode through the café, turning on lights as she went. The same small surge of pride opening always gave her pause. She'd worked so hard for this, accomplished so much, despite the horrific circumstances that had brought her to Florida in the first place. She didn't want to give it up. For the first time since she'd moved, thoughts of leaving and going home didn't bring the usual wave of relief. She was already home. And she'd be damned if anyone was going to chase her away from her home. She'd already been down that road with Bradley, and never again would she allow someone else to determine her fate.

She dropped her purse into her bottom desk drawer and rummaged through the top drawer for an elastic band. A faint trace of the smoke smell still lingered despite the shower she'd taken at Savannah's and the clean clothes she now wore. A pair of Savannah's leggings, which were a good couple inches shorter on Gia, and one of Joey's button-down shirts thrown over a camisole top and cinched with a thin belt. Not her usual work attire but functional, and it didn't stink like smoke.

But her hair still did. She smoothed it back into a knot at the back of her head and tied it up. She'd have to try lemon juice later and see if she could get the smell out. Hopefully, the groomer at the doggie day care center would have better luck getting the smell out of Thor's fur.

A quick glance at the clock told her she'd have to hurry if she was going to sit and enjoy a cup of coffee with Earl before she opened. And she was looking forward to those few minutes of peace and caffeine. Thankfully, it was a Wednesday morning and not a weekend. Wednesdays tended to be somewhat slow. Who knew? Maybe people preferred to eat breakfast at home midweek.

She moved automatically through her morning routine, her thoughts still caught up with Maybelle and Floyd Masters. Maybe Maybelle was having an affair with him. Hank was obviously straying; maybe Maybelle was too. Gia shivered at the reminder that Hank Sanford still roamed free somewhere. He and Hunt had obviously gone at it.

Hunt. She couldn't help but wonder if he was okay. She had gotten to know him fairly well over the past few months. At least, she'd thought she had. His behavior of late had her second-guessing herself.

She slid several breakfast pies into the oven to warm. She'd have to make up a few more later, but for now she'd have enough to fill the glass cake dishes on the counter, for any to-go customers. She'd found catering to people who didn't have time to sit and linger over breakfast had generated a bit more income than she'd originally thought it would when Willow had first suggested the idea. The kid had a good head on her shoulders. Gia had been tempted to teach her how to cook, but she was a natural with the customers, and Gia didn't have the heart to take that away from her.

She glanced at the clock. Willow should be there any minute, and Earl was probably already waiting out front. She finished up by lining trays of bacon, sausage, and biscuits along the back of the grill, making it easy to grab what she needed, then heated the home fries and grits and poured them into warming trays she kept on the counter. Anything to move things along more quickly and efficiently.

She checked off everything on her mental to-do list and washed her hands. Then, satisfied that everything would be okay in her absence, at least for a few minutes, she went to open the door for Earl.

She didn't make it halfway to the front door before laughter echoed through the empty café. A lot of laughter. Definitely not just Earl this morning. When she reached the door, she unlocked it and pulled it open.

Earl greeted her with a huge smile and the fisherman's cap he always wore clutched in both hands against his chest. "Mornin', Gia."

"Good morning, Earl."

The large group gathered around him ranged in age from infants to middle-aged adults.

"Are these people with you?"

He puffed up. "Yes, ma'am. All my young 'uns are in town for a visit, and I thought I'd treat them all to breakfast. I hope it's not too much."

She couldn't disappoint him no matter how exhausted she was. "Of course it's not too much. Come on in."

"Oh, you don't have to seat us early. I don't mind waiting."

"Don't be silly." She stepped back, held the door open, and ushered them in. All twenty-eight of them, by her count as they rushed past. Willow would be there soon enough, and it would be easier for her to get the huge order started before she technically opened for business anyway. She left the door unlocked for Willow and followed them to the far side of the café. "You can pull the tables together along the side wall and make one big table if you'd like."

Earl gestured to several of the boys and men, who immediately set to work rearranging the café. The boisterous bunch might have been a lot to take after the night she'd had, but their laughter and enthusiasm proved just the opposite, giving her just the boost she'd been hoping to get from several cups of caffeine. Oh, right. Caffeine. How could she have forgotten to start the coffeepots? "Excuse me a minute while I get the coffee going, and I'll come back with menus."

"Sure thing." Earl dropped his hat on a window ledge and took the empty seat at the head of the table.

Gia started all the pots lining the counter, then grabbed a stack of menus and an order pad and returned to the table.

"I'll take those." Earl reached for the stack of menus, took one off the top, then passed the rest down the line. He winked at Gia. "Easier that way."

She laughed. She'd liked Earl the moment she'd met him, and her fondness for him had only grown stronger over the past months. She leaned close to his ear. "You were certainly right."

"I usually am," he laughed, "but about what specifically?"

"This is quite a legacy your Heddie left behind." She gestured down the table at the bunch he'd brought in. Children helped each other read the menus, adults settled kids with toys that appeared out of bags, men and women chatted and laughed. One big happy family. A family any man would be proud of. The kind of family Gia so desperately wanted.

She shook off the thought. Where had that even come from? She'd found herself thinking a lot about family since she'd come to Florida. Having grown up without her mother and with a father who'd tossed her out the day she graduated from high school, Gia had never known the joy of being a part of anything like Earl's family. Or Savannah's.

Tears shimmered in the corner of Earl's eyes. "Why yes it is, thank you."

Gia laid a hand on his shoulder and squeezed. "So, do you eat your usual breakfast when you're out with the kids?"

"He sure does," a boy of about fourteen yelled from the other end of the table. "Dad says the old goat eats like a horse."

Laughter erupted from most of the family, but a woman with the same dark curls as the boy stood and leaned over the table, then spoke to him in a hushed whisper Gia couldn't quite make out.

"Oh, leave him alone, Sally." Earl thumped his chest. "This old goat does eat like a horse."

That brought more laughter and jeering, and the boy smirked—but had the good grace to cover it with a hand and pretend to cough.

His mother's warning glare told Gia she was having none of it.

"Okay, then, let's see what everyone else wants." Gia moved down the line taking orders. Earl introduced each person when she took their orders—the dark-haired boy with the smart mouth was named Earl for his grandfather. It seemed appropriate somehow. Gia would never remember all their names, never mind put names to faces. So she settled for keeping the orders straight.

Willow strode through the door and stopped short. She looked back and forth between the large group and the clock.

"This is Earl's family," Gia explained. "They are all in for a visit."

Willow smiled. "Oh, that's so nice. It's great to meet all of you."

Leaving Willow to serve coffee and drinks, Gia retreated to the kitchen. She tacked up the row of order slips and got started. No way could she fit everything on the grill at once, so she'd have to do a few orders at a time. She scrambled two dozen eggs and spilled them onto the grill, lined bacon and sausage behind the eggs, and filled all the toasters with bread.

"Gia?" Willow hurried through the door a few minutes later and tacked six more slips up. "Are you going to be able to handle all of this?"

"I've got it. What's going on out there? Why the big crowd?" She lined plates along the counter and started filling them with eggs, bacon, and toast, adding generous helpings of home fries. Seems the younger Dennisons didn't share their elder's enthusiasm for grits. Not that she blamed them.

"The orders I just put up are for a group of firemen. Apparently, they were up all night fighting a fire in your neck of the woods."

"Yes, they were. Saved my house too."

Willow started for the doorway.

"Hey, do me a favor?" Gia called after her.

Willow stopped and looked back. "What's up?"

"Don't leave the firemen a check. Tell them I said thank you."

"You got it."

"Oh, and take twenty-five percent off Earl's bill."

She nodded and hurried back to the dining room.

Gia stared at the order, only slightly overwhelmed, mostly because she was so exhausted. If she had a cook, Gia could just pitch in in the kitchen for a while, help out through the worst of the rush, and still be able to take a minute to interact with Earl's family and thank the firemen herself. As it was... Well, she'd be lucky to bang the orders out in a reasonable amount of time.

She moved several plates to the cutout for Willow to grab and took a quick peek into the dining room.

Several more tables were filled, and Willow rushed around trying to get everyone coffee or orange juice and take orders.

As Gia started to turn back, her attention caught on a man seated in the back of the café, not hidden in shadow but closer to the counter than he'd been the day before, since Earl's family had taken up the whole side wall.

He was younger than she'd originally thought, though still probably in his sixties, his face appearing to be lined more by stress than age. Deep furrows marred his brow and bracketed his mouth. He sat rigid, his gaze firmly riveted on the front door. His menu sat closed on the table in front of him.

The smell of something burning reached her. She whirled toward the toasters just in time to see a small wisp of smoke. Just what she needed, another fire. She popped the toast up and tossed the burnt pieces in the trash, then had to start over.

"Knock, knock." An older man, his salt-and-pepper hair hanging just past his Hawaiian print shirt collar, poked his head into the kitchen. "Got a minute?"

"Um..." She used her arm to wipe the sweat standing over the hot grill brought from her forehead and yanked down the order slips she'd just finished, then moved the others in line down, making room for the four more Willow rushed in and tacked up.

"I'm sorry. I can see you're busy, and I wouldn't interrupt if it weren't of the utmost importance." His soft-spoken manner made it impossible for her to blow him off. "My name is Cole Barrister."

"No problem. It's a pleasure to meet you, Mr. Barrister, I'm Gia Morelli."

"It's nice to meet you as well. Please, call me Cole."

"Sorry I can't stop and shake hands, I'm just a bit swamped this morning." She gestured toward a stool in the far corner. "Please. Pull the stool up and have a seat. As long as you can talk while I work, I can give you a few minutes."

"Of course, of course. Thank you." He pulled the stool closer, but stayed far enough out of the way for her to work. He chuckled softly. "I remember these days. Sometimes even fondly."

"You were a cook?"

"Of sorts. I worked grill at a stand on the beach for many, many years."

"Did you cook breakfast?"

"Among other things."

"What do you do now?" She cut several pieces of meat lover's pie and put them on plates with home fries, then put the plates on the cutout and rang the bell. She took a quick peek into the dining room.

The older man sat sipping a cup of coffee, his menu still closed on the table.

"A little of this, a little of that," Cole said. "I retired about five years back."

"Well, good for you."

"I suppose."

"Don't you like being retired?" She checked the next order slip.

"To be honest, it's not all it's cracked up to be. I'm actually quite bored."

"Really?" Retiring in Florida seemed like a dream come true. And yet, she couldn't imagine what she'd do all day long if she ever retired.

"What can I say? I'm a glutton for punishment. A man can only visit so many theme parks, spend so many days sitting on the beach, and read so many books. Watching you right now, I actually miss the rush." He laughed, a deep belly laugh, surprising for a man with such a soft voice. "I must be crazy, right?"

"Maybe, but that's okay. I think I'd probably be bored if I ever stopped working too." She counted the number of eggs she needed for sandwiches and cracked them onto the grill, then broke the yolks. "But... I may have an idea that would be mutually beneficial for both of us."

"Okay, you've piqued my interest."

"In case you couldn't tell, I am in desperate need of a cook." She gestured toward the full grill and the row of order tickets fluttering above it, demanding her attention.

"Oh, I don't—"

She held up a hand to stop him, and an egg dropped from the spatula she held and landed on the floor with a splat. She sighed and reached for the paper towels.

He grabbed them before her and cleaned up the egg.

"Thank you." He might just be exactly what she was looking for. She cracked another egg onto the grill. "It wouldn't have to be full-time. Maybe you could just pitch in on weekend mornings, when I'm usually the busiest, and a day or two during the week if you'd like?"

He contemplated the grill. "It would be nice to do something useful with my time. Can I think about it?"

"Of course. Just stop in anytime and let me know if you'd like to give it a try."

"Oh, right. Speaking of stopping in, I wanted to let you know we're organizing a community petition."

"For Boggy Creek?"

"No, for Rolling Pines." He pulled a folded sheet of printer paper out of his pocket. "I've already gotten about half the residents to sign, and I was wondering if you would too?"

"What is it for?"

"I want to go before the town council and get approval to have a fire exit put in at the back of the development." His hand shook as he held out the paper. "That fire last night was a real eye opener. If that place had gone up, there's no chance all of us would have gotten out. Especially if it had been toward the front of the development instead of the back."

Gia shivered, despite the heat pouring off the grill. "Absolutely, I'll sign."

"Thank you." He held out a pen. "Signatures are a big help, but I think the more residents who show up at the meeting, the better chance we'll have of being taken seriously."

She stripped off her gloves and signed the petition, then handed it back to him. "Just let me know when the meeting is, and I'll be there."

"Thank you very much, ma'am."

"You bet. It was nice meeting you, Cole. And don't forget about the job offer."

"I won't." He waved over his shoulder on his way out the door.

Gia piled bacon and eggs on a roll, topped it with a piece of cheese, salt, pepper, and ketchup, then wrapped it and stuffed it into a bag. She put the order up in the cutout and rang the bell for Willow.

The older man was gone, his coffee cup sitting beside a rumpled linen napkin and the closed menu on the table. No way could running into him three times in less than twenty-four hours be a coincidence. Someone had to know who her mystery man was. Now if she could just escape the kitchen long enough to find that someone.

Chapter 13

Gia stretched her back, then flipped the last egg on the grill and waited for it to cook. She tilted her head from side to side. More than twelve hours in front of the grill had left her sweating and stiff. She really hoped Cole considered her offer and then agreed. She loved cooking, but she needed a break sometimes.

And she needed to find out who her stalker was. If the man she kept seeing was even looking for her. Could be he just happened to be in the restaurant the night before. Boggy Creek was a small town, and people tended to frequent the same places. And yet... Something about him made her uncomfortable.

Could he be Marcia's killer? But why would he be stalking Gia? Looking for whatever documents she'd left for her, maybe? Too bad Gia had no clue what they were about or where to find them.

"Gia?" Willow pulled off her apron and rolled it into a ball. "Everything is done out front, and I'm getting ready to head out."

"Thanks, Willow. I know it was a madhouse out there today. I'm sorry I couldn't get out front to help."

"No worries. I like it when it's busy. Makes the time fly by."

"Don't I know it." The day really had gone by in a flash. "I'll see you tomorrow."

"Yup. Good night."

Gia slid the egg onto the bacon, ham, and sausage she'd already piled on a roll, then added cheese, salt, and pepper. She scooped a generous serving of home fries into a container, then filled another with grits, and put everything in a bag with Harley's name on the front. She wished she could do more for him. Although he had problems, including the fact he couldn't seem to go inside a building, which left him homeless and wandering the streets, he was a good man with a good heart. The business owners along Main Street all watched out for him, but he'd only accept so much help. She'd offered him use of the empty apartment over the café, but as far as she could tell, he'd never taken her up on it.

She poured a large sweet tea, put the cover on with a piece of tape to hold it down, tossed a straw, napkins, and utensils into his bag, and set everything on the counter. Even though she'd already finished cleaning up, and Willow never forgot to do anything, Gia double-checked everything was clean and ready to open the next day as she hurried through and grabbed the stack of newspapers from behind the register. She'd already had Willow rip the covers off to return to the company, so Gia carried the rest to the back to leave for Harley, who used them to keep warm in the winter.

Gia pushed the door open. Harley's dinner from the night before still sat on the small table beside the stack of newspapers she'd left. Weird. Harley had been taking dinner since she'd first started leaving it. She added the papers she held to the stack, tossed the old food in the garbage, and set the new food out. She squinted and tried to peer into the woods, but she couldn't see any sign of him in the shadows. Hopefully, he was okay.

She pulled the door closed, locked it, grabbed her purse from her office, and took one last look around. Finally done. She was about ready to fall on her face. She thought about making a quick cup of coffee to take with her, but her stomach churned. No sleep, swamped all day, all she wanted was a hot shower and her bed.

Digging through her purse for the keys, she practically ran toward the front door.

"Excuse me."

Gia jumped at the deep, unfamiliar voice.

A man she'd never seen before stood just inside the door, wearing a blue uniform and holding a large white envelope in his hand. "I'm sorry. I didn't mean to startle you. I'm with Rapid Couriers, and I have a package for you."

"Oh." Gia gave a nervous laugh as she pressed the hand holding her key ring against her chest and stabbed herself with a key. She dropped the keys back into her bag and rubbed the sore spot. "I'm sorry. It's been a very long day."

"No problem, ma'am. The door was open, but I didn't see anyone so I figured I'd just come in and wait." He held the envelope out to her.

"Thank you." It was her own fault; she should have walked out front and locked the door when Willow had left. You'd think she'd have learned that lesson already. She couldn't even think clearly. It was time to go home before she collapsed somewhere. She dug a few dollar bills out of her bag, handed them to him, and took the letter.

"Thank you, ma'am." He tipped his hat and left.

She contemplated the envelope for a moment. Her name and address were neatly printed across the front, but there were no other markings and no return address. Exhaustion won out over curiosity. She probably wouldn't be able to read the words anyway. Already, the world appeared as nothing more than a blurry haze. Time to go.

She dropped the letter into her bag and locked up, then turned and stood on the walkway, staring at the empty spot where she usually parked her car. How could she have forgotten Savannah had driven her to work? Tears leaked out the corners of her eyes.

Gia pulled out her phone and dialed Savannah's number as she walked toward the doggie day care center to pick up Thor. Thankfully, it wasn't that far, and the cool evening air helped clear her mind a little.

Savannah picked up on the second ring. "Hey. Ready to go?"

"Go where?"

"Home, silly. I'm just taking care of my dogs, and I'll be there to pick you up."

She should have realized Savannah would come back for her. "Sorry, Savannah, it's been a long day."

"I bet."

"Have you heard anything from Hunt?" Gia asked.

"No. Have you?"

"Nothing." And she was worried sick about him. But she didn't have to tell Savannah that; the concern was already evident in Savannah's voice.

"I'm about done with the dogs. Where are you now?"

"I'm headed to pick up Thor." The thought of the long ride home was too much to contemplate. "You know what?"

"What?"

"Don't even worry about picking me up. I think I'll take a walk in the park with Thor, hit one of the food trucks for dinner, and crash at the apartment."

"Are you sure?" Savannah asked.

"Yeah, I have no idea what's going on up there. I did hear the fire was out, but I don't feel like dealing with anything else tonight. I just want to close my eyes." Everything she owned probably smelled like smoke anyway. No sense going home tonight, when she was too tired to do anything. After a good night's sleep, she could go home and deal with laundry and whatever else needed doing.

"Aww, honey. I understand. Do you need anything?"

"I could use some clothes to wear tomorrow."

"No problem. I'll drop something off to you later."

"Thanks, Savannah."

"Of course. What are friends for?"

Gia disconnected and dropped the phone back into her bag. The cool air against her face felt good, but the humidity still made breathing feel a little too much like work. She strolled down Main Street, taking her time, enjoying the small-town feel.

Kids rode by her on bikes, parents pushed strollers, couples walked hand in hand, and not one of them seemed to be in a hurry. The leisurely pace at which everyone in Boggy Creek moved forced Gia to slow down, to enjoy life instead of rushing through it without experiencing much of anything. And she loved it. She loved everything about it. The slower pace brought a sense of peace she'd never known, even in her current state of exhaustion.

"Gia." Trevor ran over from across the street. "Hold up."

"Hey, Trevor."

"Hi." He tripped over the curb and would have gone flat on his face if not for a nice save by one of the palm trees lining the street. He pushed away from the tree and smoothed a hand over his shirt. "As I was saying. Hi, Gia."

She couldn't help laughing, even though she'd come to expect his clumsiness. "How in the world do you stay up on a paddleboard for hours yet trip over your own feet trying to walk?"

His adorable grin could light up the darkest mood. "It's a gift."

"Obviously." The one time he'd taken her paddleboarding, she'd been amazed by his skill.

"So, you headed over to get Thor?"

"Yes. I forgot Savannah dropped me off this morning, so I don't have a car. I figured I'd head over to the park, then crash at the apartment. I didn't get much sleep last night."

"I heard about the fire. I'm sorry. Did you lose much?"

"I don't think I lost anything, but I haven't been home all day."

"If you need a ride, I'd be happy to take you."

Though the thought of her nice comfy bed did appeal, she could get an extra hour of sleep if she just stayed at the apartment. She needed the hour. Of course, if Hunt showed up battered and bruised again, she wouldn't be there. Plus, she had told Harley he could use the apartment whenever he wanted. Not that he ever had. Thinking hurt her brain. "I'm good, Trevor, thank you."

"No problem. I'll walk with you to the day care center, but then I have to get back."

She started walking along the sidewalk side by side with Trevor. She'd thought about stopping by his shop earlier, but walking together worked out even better. Multitasking at its best. "Have you seen Harley lately?"

"No, why?"

"I don't know. I left his dinner out yesterday, and he didn't take it. Didn't take the newspapers either."

"That is weird. I haven't seen him, but I'll certainly ask around and see if anyone else has."

"Thanks, Trevor. I worry about him."

"I know. Me too. But everyone around here looks out for him. I'm sure he'll be okay. He's probably just roaming around somewhere being... well, Harley."

"I guess, but I'd feel better if I knew someone had seen him."

"Have you checked the clearing in the woods?"

"No, it was late when I realized he hadn't eaten last night's dinner." She left off the fact she rarely, if ever, went out to the back parking lot except to dump the garbage.

It didn't matter. The look of sympathy he offered when he squeezed her hand told her he understood. "I'll let you know if I hear anything."

"Thanks." If his bag was still there when she got up the next morning, she'd have to suck it up and check the clearing he often hung out in on the far side of her parking lot. If she looked straight ahead, she'd probably be able to avoid looking at the dumpster. And if she couldn't, well, she'd just have to deal with it. She owed Harley that much. He'd been a good friend to her, and nothing would stop her from being there for him.

When they reached the day care center, they stopped. "Well, I'm going to head back now. We're still on for Monday, right?"

"Monday?"

"Kayaking?"

"Sure thing. I'm looking forward to it." *In a not so excited about getting in a flimsy little boat in a lake full of critters sort of way.*

"Great." He started backing away. "I'll see you Monday morning, then. Unless I see you sooner, which I might, since we only work a few stores down from each other."

He backed into a bench and plopped down to sit. "I meant to do that."

Gia laughed as she waved and hurried in to pick up Thor.

* * * *

After sitting in the park and having two tacos and a large Diet Pepsi, Gia returned to the apartment above the café, fed Thor and took him for one last walk, then locked up. A clean pair of leggings and a tunic style top lay over a chair at the small round table in the corner of the kitchen. Apparently, Savannah had already come and gone.

The idea of a hot shower flickered into her mind, then flickered right back out again as she flopped onto the couch and dropped her head back. The minute she landed, her eyes started to close.

She lifted her purse, which she'd tossed onto the couch on her way in, and dropped it onto the floor. The white envelope the courier had brought fell out and slid across the laminate flooring. She had half a mind to leave it by the side of the couch where it landed, but no matter how tired she was, the curiosity wouldn't allow her to sleep until she knew what it contained. Better to just open it and get it over with.

She snagged the envelope beneath her bare foot and pulled it toward her across the floor. Curiosity did not give her the energy to get up. She picked it up, ripped it open, and pulled out a single sheet of printer paper.

Dear Ms. Morelli,

I was so sorry to hear your establishment would be closing. If you are interested in selling, I would be pleased if you would consider my offer.

She turned the page over, but other than the short paragraph followed by a ridiculously low offer and a corporate stamp with a signature she couldn't read scribbled above it, nothing gave any indication where the letter had come from. It had to be some sort of joke. She couldn't make out the signature, but the stamp was from a company called the Starboard Corporation. She'd never heard of it. Of course, she didn't have her computer with her, so she couldn't even look it up. She tossed the letter aside and lay down on the couch.

Thor lay on the floor beside her. She didn't have a crate for him at the apartment, but he'd have to make do.

Her eyes fell shut and she drifted in and out, on the verge of sleep, but not quite there. The smell of smoke wafted to her. Flames flickered against the backs of her eyelids. Light, dark, light, dark, a dizzying array of color and shadow. The crackle and pop as the flames consumed everything in their path. She was trapped. Nowhere to go. No escape. A wall of flames and heat battered her, threatened to consume her.

She jerked upright and took a huge gulp of air. Clean air. No smoke. No flames. Just Thor snoring softly at her side. She grabbed her cell phone and checked the time. Three AM. No way could she call anyone now, but first thing in the morning, she'd call Savannah and ask her to see if Tommy would allow her to come before the town council and beg for a fire exit in Rolling Pines.

Chapter 14

When the alarm went off Monday morning, Gia hit the snooze button. Kayaking day had arrived faster than she would have thought possible, especially considering she hadn't had a decent night's sleep in almost a week. Plagued by nightmares, concerned about Harley, who no one had seen in close to a week despite Gia working up the courage to check the clearing behind the café, sick with worry over Hunt, who she hadn't seen or heard from since the night of the fire, Gia spent most nights lying awake, staring at the ceiling—which whoever had painted missed a spot just above the bed. When she wasn't trying to sleep, she spent her time scrubbing the smoky stench from everything in the house, washing all the curtains, linens, clothing, and shampooing the area rugs. She was just grateful there was no damage.

The alarm went off again, and she had half a mind to call Trevor and tell him she couldn't go. What would be a good enough excuse to get out of paddling a thin wisp of a boat through snake and alligator infested waters? Anything! But there was no excuse good enough to hurt Trevor.

The third time the alarm sounded, she swung her feet over the side of the bed and sat up. She turned the alarm off, stood, and slid her feet into her slippers. "Come on, boy. If I have to be up, you have to be up too."

Thor moaned and stood, then stretched his front paws and arched his back.

She trudged toward the kitchen with Thor on her heels. After starting a pot of coffee, she opened the back door to let Thor out. He was halfway through the door when Gia spotted the snake on the deck and snagged his collar. "Wait, Thor."

She yanked him back and slammed the French door all in one motion, then peeked out the window. A long, thick snake lay curled in a puddle of sunlight on the deck right outside the door. She started to hyperventilate. She had no idea what kind of snake it was, just that some of them could be poisonous. On the bright side, she was now wide awake.

Thor whined at her side, fidgeting around, pacing back and forth in front of the door.

"All right, boy. Hold on."

First things first. She had to get him out before he had an accident on the floor. But no way was she going out back, and neither was Thor. She grabbed her cell phone, clipped Thor's leash to his collar, and headed for the front door. She opened it and peered out. Nothing seemed amiss. Of course, anything could be lurking in the woods, or the grass, or just out of sight in the early morning shadows. "Go fast, Thor."

She hurried him out, searched everywhere at once while he took *forever* to go, then ran back in and slammed the door. Then locked it for good measure. You never could be too safe. She dialed Hunt's number. As expected, he didn't pick up. She didn't bother to leave a message; she'd already left about ten, and the last time she'd called, an electronic voice had informed her that his voice mailbox was full.

So she called Savannah.

"Hey, there." If the grogginess in her voice was any indication, Gia had woken her. "What are you doing up so early on your day off?"

"Well, I'm supposed to be going kayaking, but I have a problem."

"What kind of problem?"

"There's a giant snake on my back deck."

"Giant?"

How dare she sound so skeptical?

"Well, it's really big. What am I supposed to do?"

"Leave it alone and go kayaking."

Was she out of her mind? "And what happens when I come home. I have to let Thor out. I can't let him out there knowing that thing could be lurking anywhere. And what if it's poisonous?"

"Calm down, Gia. Take a deep breath."

Okay. She did have to admit she'd worked herself up into a bit of a tizzy, but in her defense, it was a pretty big snake.

"What color is the snake?"

"I don't know." She ran to the kitchen and looked out the door. Sure enough, he was still there sunning himself as if he owned the place. "It's blackish brown, has kind of like patches on it."

"Hang up and take a picture of it, then post it in the community page and see if anyone can identify it and maybe relocate it for you."

"Relo—are you nuts? How do you know it won't find its way back?"

"Have them relocate it really, really far away. Now, if you're okay, I'm going back to sleep, because I'm off today too, and I'm not going anywhere this early."

"Are you really going to—"

Savannah disconnected.

Okay, she'd do as Savannah suggested. She took a picture of the snake, which hadn't moved an inch since she'd found it. Crazy as it seemed, she considered that a good thing. If that monster disappeared, she'd probably never go outside again. Never mind the fact there was probably a whole family—or flock, or herd, or whatever you called a bunch of snakes—roaming, or slithering as the case may be, all over the place out there.

She tried to ignore her fear while she posted the picture in the Boggy Creek Community group along with a plea for help *relocating* it. Then she fed Thor, keeping one eye on the offending creature to make sure he didn't disappear.

Thor finished eating and looked up at her. Of course, he had to go out again.

She grabbed a paper towel and mopped the sweat from her brow. "Okay, boy. We're going to go out the front again, and you have to make it fast."

Thor tilted his head, and his tongue lolled out the side of his mouth.

Taking that for acknowledgment, she clipped his leash on and dug the bear spray out of her purse. Who knew? It might work on snakes. She grabbed a plastic bag from a basket in the laundry room and headed out.

She had to walk farther away from the house this time for Thor to find a spot he liked. Figured he'd choose that moment to be picky. As soon as she passed the shelter of the porch, the smell from the fire hit her. Maybe that's why the snake was camped out on her deck. Perhaps his home had been burned. She walked down the driveway, where at least she'd see a snake before she got within striking distance. She hoped.

A large section of woods had been blackened by the flames. Though scorched, her garage hadn't sustained any substantial damage. She'd been lucky. It could just have easily gone up in flames. Along with the house. If Hunt hadn't been there...

She'd have to snap a few pictures later to take to the council meeting on Tuesday. When Savannah had called Tommy and explained the situation, he had agreed to let her speak at the meeting, and she'd already contacted

Cole to let him know. Hopefully, he'd be able to get some of the community members to show up and support her.

Thor finally finished, and Gia bent to clean up the mess.

The sun glinted off something in the brush toward the end of the driveway.

After closely surveying the surrounding area for wildlife, then dropping the garbage bag into one of the bear-proof pails by the garage, she returned to the spot she'd seen the reflection from. There it was again. She squinted and moved closer, bear spray at the ready.

A cell phone lay in the brush on the far side of the driveway. Gia picked it up.

"Hey, there." A man walked down the road toward her carrying a metal rake and a large bucket.

"Hi." She waved.

"I'm Scott Harper." He gestured over his shoulder. "I live just next door."

Thor squirmed a little but stayed put.

"Who's this big fella?" Scott petted Thor's head.

"This is Thor, and I'm Gia."

"Pleasure to meet you, Gia. I saw your post in the community group and came to see if you still needed help."

"Oh, yes. Thank you. And thank you for coming over to help the night of the fire. I saw you, but I never got a chance to say hello or thank you for your help."

"Anytime. We've got to stick together out here and help each other out. Speaking of, where is he?"

"Out back." She started toward the house, then paused, not entirely comfortable inviting a strange man into her house. Then again, the snake wasn't going to relocate itself, and if it did, it might not be far enough away. "Come on. You can go through the house."

Scott followed her inside and through to the kitchen. She unclipped Thor's leash and draped it over a chair. "It's right out those doors."

Scott looked out the window. "Yup. Just what I expected. I couldn't really see the head on the picture you posted, but I had my suspicions."

"You know what kind of snake it is?"

"A cottonmouth."

"Cottonmouth?"

"Some people call 'em water moccasins. Either way, you don't want to get bit by one of those babies."

"They're poisonous?"

"Yup. You can tell by the triangular shape of the head." Scott pointed and traced a triangle in the air around the outline of the snake's head.

At least now she'd have a way to recognize one if she ever came across it again.

Scott gripped the doorknob.

Gia grabbed his arm to keep him from opening the door. "You won't let it get in, right?"

He patted her hand, amusement sparkling in his kind eyes. "Don't worry. It won't get in. Promise."

She nodded and stepped back, clinging tightly to Thor's collar so he wouldn't charge through the doorway with Scott. "And you'll relocate it really far away, right? Like, really, really far away. So he can't find his way back?"

Scott laughed out loud, his cheeks turning bright red with the strain. "Don't you worry, ma'am. I'll relocate him too far away for him to ever find his way back."

"Thank you." She shut the door behind him and watched him take the lid off the bucket, scoop the monster up with the rake and drop it in the bucket, then slap the lid back on nice and tight.

When he opened the door and walked back through the house with the snake, she kept her gaze firmly riveted on the top of the bucket. She didn't even blink until he was out the front door and standing on the porch. And even then, she kept one eye on the bucket. "Thank you again, Scott. I can't tell you how much I appreciate you coming over to help. If you're ever in town and you'd like to come into the All-Day Breakfast Café, I'll treat you to breakfast."

"That sounds great. My wife has been saying she wants to have breakfast there. All the women in her book club talk about how great the food is."

"Thank you. I'd be happy to treat you and your wife."

"Why, thank you, ma'am." He nodded once and left.

Gia closed the door behind him, turned around, and leaned her back against the door. Though having the snake gone did bring some relief, she wasn't sure she'd ever feel comfortable walking out the door again. On the other hand, Scott Harper had come to her rescue only minutes after her plea for help. She'd have to call it a tie. One big, fat check in the minus column for the snake and one in the plus column for Scott. Of course, she could give Scott two checks—one for removing the snake and the other for taking it very far away—and tip the scales in favor of staying. Then again, the snake was not only a snake but poisonous too. Tie again. Of course, Scott got a plus for helping put out the fire too.

She sighed and shoved away from the door. If she didn't get ready soon, she was going to be late. Wouldn't want to be late for kayaking. As if she hadn't already witnessed her fair share of wildlife this morning.

She started toward the bathroom, then remembered the cell phone she'd found and detoured to the kitchen. She'd go nuts without her phone. The least she could do was let whomever it belonged to know she'd found it.

Maybe one of the firemen had dropped it. Or one of the police officers who'd also responded. She pushed the button and the home screen popped up—no password required. She brought up the contact list and scrolled through for a familiar name or something labeled *Home, Hubby, Mom, Dad,* anything that would give her a place to call.

She stopped when she reached the name Floyd. Coincidence? Probably not. No last name had been listed, but how many Floyds could there be in Boggy Creek? She continued scrolling, searching for any more familiar names. She passed her own name. Then Hank.

That was enough. With no doubt in her mind it was Maybelle's phone, she hit the button to return to the home screen. She'd have to give the phone to the police. It proved Maybelle had been on her property, if nothing else. Very close to where the fire had started. But wouldn't the police and fire investigators have searched the area the night of the fire? The trampled grass surrounding it made it seem impossible they'd have missed the phone lying where it was.

Which could only mean one of two things. Either everyone had somehow managed to miss the phone lying on the ground in a spot they must have walked over a hundred times. Or, Maybelle had come back after the fire.

Gia only debated for a fraction of a second before bringing up the call log. The way she figured it, the phone was found on her property, which made it fair game. She needn't have bothered. The history was blank. Either Maybelle didn't speak to anyone by phone, which Gia found hard to believe considering Hank must have called her for a ride—of course, he could have called the house—or Maybelle had deleted her call history.

Gia dialed Hunt's number and got the same result she'd gotten the last few hundred times she'd tried. No answer. Full voicemail box. She disconnected and dialed Leo.

"Hey, Gia, what's up?"

"I'm not sure, but I think I found Maybelle's cell phone in the brush beside my driveway."

"What makes you think it's hers?"

"I scrolled through the contacts and it seemed like people Maybelle would know."

"All right, hang tight, make sure your doors are locked, and make sure you stay observant and keep your bear spray with you if you take Thor out before I get there."

"Get here?"

"To pick up the phone."

"Oh, well, I'm headed out anyway. Why don't I drop it off and save you the trip out here?" she said.

"That would be great, thanks. I'll be at the station for the next couple of hours."

"All right, I'll see you in a little while."

"See ya then."

"Wait." As much as she didn't want to put Leo in an awkward position, she had to ask.

"What's up?" he asked.

"Have you talked to Hunt at all lately?"

"Yes."

Surprised by his answer, she hesitated, unsure what she wanted to know. In the long run, only one thing really mattered. "Is he all right?"

"He's fine, Gia. He had to go out of town."

"For what?" She regretted the words the instant they left her lips. "Sorry, it's none of my business. I just—"

"It's fine, Gia. He had to follow up on a lead."

"Thanks, Leo."

"No problem. Just make sure you're careful until we get a better idea of what's going on. Two bodies in one week are more than enough."

"*Two* bodies?"

"Oh, uh…"

"Leo."

"I'm hanging up now, Gia. Gotta go dig my foot outta my mouth. Just be careful."

Chapter 15

Gia called Trevor to tell him she was running late, then got ready, dropped Thor off at day care, and dropped Maybelle's phone off with Leo—who adamantly refused to elaborate on whom the second body might belong to.

Once she'd finished procrastinating as long as she possibly could, she sat in the parking lot at the river Trevor had talked her into meeting him at and rested her head on her hands on the steering wheel. It was now or never. If she wasn't going to kayak, she may as well head on home. To her house. Where someone had started a fire and a wacko, stalker, ex-employee might be lurking in any shadow just waiting for a chance to…

To what? Gia had no clue. But she figured she might be better off braving the wildlife than going home. At least critters didn't carry guns. The memory brought an instant chill. She shivered and turned off the air conditioner. Going home wouldn't help her escape the critters. Unless it was home to New York. And New York had muggers.

A knock on her window made her jump. She whirled toward the sound. Trevor waved.

Okay. I can do this. Gia plastered on a smile, opened the door, and climbed out. "Hi?"

"Hey." Trevor backpedaled to get away from the door, tripped over a root, and regained his footing as if nothing unusual had happened. *Jeez.* And she was going into a lake full of monsters with this guy? "I got a little nervous when you didn't get out of the car right away. I thought you might have changed your mind."

"Of course not." *Definitely.* "Why would I change my mind?" *Just because I don't want to get eaten?*

"I don't know why you would, but I'm glad you didn't. You're going to love it."

Somehow she doubted that.

He held out his elbow and smiled, and she hooked her arm through his. Maybe he was afraid she'd turn tail and run if he didn't hold on to her. It seemed he knew her better than she realized.

He guided her toward the river. "I already have the kayaks in the water and tied to a downed tree. Yours is the blue one."

"Thanks." She worked hard to show some level of enthusiasm, but it wasn't easy with her stomach twisted into a knot.

"There you go." Trevor indicated two kayaks, one red, one blue, resting on the shore.

She scanned the river and the shore. No alligators that she could see. Of course, they could easily be lurking just below the surface. Maybe she should just stick to staying on land. Then again, she'd seen video of alligators running. Who'd have expected those giant, lumbering creatures could move so quickly? Okay, maybe she'd be safer in the boat.

She sucked in a deep breath, the humidity weighing heavily on her chest, and wiped the sweat from her brow with a shaky hand. "Is it always this hot here in the winter?"

"Not always. This is actually a really warm winter. They're talking about severe storms later, though."

"Storms?"

"Thunderstorms. A cold front is supposed to come through." Trevor leaned over her kayak and grabbed a long paddle with two flattened ends. He held it out to her.

"It gets cold here?"

"Oh, yeah. Sometimes really cold. Especially overnight, but it usually warms up quick enough once the sun comes out."

It wasn't too late to run for it. Instead, she held her hand out and took the paddle. "Thanks."

To his credit, Trevor refrained from commenting on how badly her hand trembled. He moved behind her and reached around her with both arms. He tilted the paddle horizontal and guided her hands into position to hold the paddle properly. "You hold it with your hands apart, like this. Make sure you have it right side up, with the concave side facing you. Line your knuckles up with the top edge of the blade. Hold it about a foot in front of you. Then you alternate one side," he said as he guided the paddle through a stroke as if in the water, then repeated the motion in the opposite direction, "and the other side. It's easy once you get the hang of it. You just need to get a smooth rhythm going. And don't just use your arms, you're going to twist your body a bit with each stroke."

He guided her through a few more strokes, then stepped back. "You try it."

"Okay." She tried it on her own.

"That's it."

It didn't seem too hard.

He bounced up and down, clearly excited to get started. "Got it?"

"I think so." While standing on dry land anyway. Once she had to balance herself in the kayak and stroke through water, who knew?

"Great." A huge grin lit up his face. "Let's go."

She looked out over the lake's smooth surface. She could do this. Trevor was as clumsy as a bull in a china shop, at least, according to Savannah. If he could kayak, she could too. She followed Trevor to the kayak, and he waded into the water. "You want to hold the kayak parallel to the shoreline. I'll hold it for you this time."

"Thanks," she muttered, trying to concentrate on getting into the boat he held tilted for her to get in. She got one foot in okay, but balancing herself while she pulled the second leg in proved challenging, and she tipped the kayak.

Thankfully, Trevor kept her from flipping it upside down and ending up fully submerged. "Try again."

She groaned but gave it another go. Her second attempt went a bit smoother, and she ended up sitting in the kayak with the paddle held across the front of the boat.

Trevor backed away an inch at a time, his hands held at the ready in case she went over. "Are you okay if I get in my kayak now?"

She nodded, careful not to move too much and flip herself over. "I think so."

"Don't worry, you'll get it. We'll go nice and slow for a while." He climbed into his own kayak with all the grace, skill, and balance of a gymnast. Go figure. He maneuvered the kayak beside her, but not too close. Maybe kayakers were supposed to keep some distance between them. Or maybe he just didn't want to get dunked if she went ass over teakettle.

She sat for a moment, trying to orient herself to the smooth rocking motion the gentle current caused. At first, she thought she was going to flip every time she moved. Within a few minutes, she began to gain confidence. As long as she was sitting still, anyway.

"You okay?" Trevor yelled.

"Yup." She gripped the paddle exactly as he'd shown her, took care to line her knuckles up with the blade, held it out in front of her, and dipped one end into the water. The kayak started to tip as it spun toward Trevor. She jammed the paddle into the sandy bottom, halting any movement.

"Try again. You'll get it."

Just what she needed, a cheerleader. She huffed out a breath. Trevor was just trying to help, and he was such a sweet friend, but he might just have to accept she wasn't the outdoors type. She glanced at him. "So, how do you like bowling?"

"I don't know. I've never gone," he said.

"You've never gone bowling?"

"Nope."

"Would you like to?"

"Sure. I'd love to give it a try sometime."

"I was thinking we could go now."

Trevor laughed. "You can do it. Just take your time and try again."

Gia managed to maneuver the kayak around until she was facing the same direction as Trevor.

"The rest is easy. Just use the paddle the way I showed you."

She dipped one end into the water and dragged it back.

"Don't forget to twist your body," Trevor called.

"Got it." She tried again, this time twisting her body as she pulled through the water. Definitely a little easier that time.

"You're doing great." Trevor stayed close, but not too close, giving her room to figure out a comfortable pace.

She moved slowly at first, her strokes tentative. But as she started to move, her confidence grew. Her pace became steadier, her strokes more rhythmic. Staying balanced proved easier than she'd expected. "Hey, I think I'm getting the hang of this."

"Do you like it?"

She tore her gaze from the ends of the paddle dipping into the water and chanced a quick look around while still paddling. They weren't far from shore, sort of skirting the edges of the river as if Trevor realized she wouldn't be comfortable out in the middle of all that water. She faltered, missing a stroke.

"You got it?" he yelled.

"Yes, I'm okay. Just got a little distracted." Roots tangled together above the surface, and trees grew right up out of the water at the river's edge, soaring into the brilliant blue sky. Fluffy white clouds towered overhead. Moss hung from branches, palm trees grew wild in the surrounding woods, and beautiful flowers bloomed everywhere. "I can't get over how green everything is down here. How alive. New York in winter is pretty much bland. The sky is gray a good part of the time. If we get snow, it's beautiful while it's falling and the city is shut down, but then reality sets in, and they plow it into disgusting, sludge-filled piles lining the streets, covering the sidewalks so you barely have room to walk without ruining your shoes."

Right now, at this moment, drifting gently along the lake, cocooned in the sun's rays, she didn't miss New York. Possibly for the first time, she felt at home. "Okay, you win."

"Win what?"

"I love kayaking."

"Yes." He pumped his fist. "I knew it. I knew you'd love it."

"What's not to love? I've never felt peace like this before. It might just be my new favorite thing."

"Wow. If I knew you'd love it that much, I'd have taken you months ago."

"I'm not sure I could have fully appreciated it months ago." She been too wrapped up in Bradley's death and the subsequent investigation to find any real enjoyment in her surroundings.

Something moved in the water to her right.

She jerked to the side, rocking the kayak, then held her breath as she waited to tip. As soon as she stilled, the kayak balanced out.

A large, not-so-scary-looking turtle swam beside her, his little legs pumping wildly.

Something tan scampered amongst the interlaced roots along the shoreline. "Is that a monkey?"

"Yup. I was hoping we'd see them today. I knew you'd enjoy them."

"Oh my gosh. They're beautiful." She tried to slow the kayak to watch the group of monkeys climb and jump through the roots. One scampered up a tree and out onto a branch sticking out over her kayak. She laughed. "I didn't realize all these monkeys lived in Florida."

"Actually, they didn't originally. They escaped a tourist attraction back in the thirties, and thrived in the forest."

She drifted along the sapphire river, watching them play. "What kind of trees are those, with the roots all woven together above the water?"

"Mangroves."

"They're gorgeous. I've never seen anything like that before."

When the group of monkeys ran off out of sight, she resumed paddling. "This is truly amazing, Trevor. Thank you so much for taking me."

"Anytime." He smiled and looked around at the forest. "It's always nice coming here with someone who's never seen it before. Makes you appreciate the beauty of it all the more, as if seeing it for the first time."

"I can't imagine ever getting tired of this."

"Me neither. I've been coming here for as long as I can remember, and it never gets old or boring."

Gia caught movement from the shore in her peripheral vision. Hoping to see more monkeys, she slowed the kayak.

A woman stood on the shore, perfectly still, staring across the river as if in a trance. She leaned heavily on the long walking stick she held upright beside her. Her full-length, hooded cloak hung limply in the dampness. Not just any woman. It was the same mysterious elderly woman she'd run into the day she'd found Marcia's body.

If Gia could just talk to her, maybe get her to go into the police station and tell Captain Hayes she'd seen Gia moments before Gia had found Marcia's body, he'd have to leave her alone. He might not stop coming into the café for free coffee, but at least he'd have to stop with his snide comments and condescending looks.

She dipped the paddle into the water and turned the kayak toward shore.

"Hey," Trevor yelled. "Where are you going?"

She spared him a quick glance and put her finger against her lips to hush him. She didn't want the woman to run off before she could speak to her.

When he realized she wasn't going to turn back, Trevor followed.

The gentle current carried her farther down the river, but she managed to get the kayak close to the marshy shoreline while still keeping the woman in sight. When she'd maneuvered as close as she could, Gia used the paddle to hold the kayak still, then just sat there, with no clue how to get out. How hard could it be?

She dug the paddle into the muck and used it to steady herself, then put the other hand on the side of the kayak and tried to stand up. The kayak tilted and dumped her onto her knees in the squishy bottom. She jumped up quickly, suddenly away of all the critters that could be lurking nearby, and scanned the area. All seemed clear.

Trevor pulled his kayak beside her and stopped. "Are you all right?"

She nodded and searched for the woman.

"What are you doing?" he whispered.

Careful to keep her voice low, she answered, "I have to get out for a minute."

He looked around, then laid his paddle across the kayak behind his seat and tilted it until he could use it to hold the kayak still. He scooted up out of the compartment the seat was in and sat on the kayak behind it, then smoothly swung his leg over and stood.

So that's how you do it. Seemed easy enough. Better than her way.

She handed him her paddle and started along the shore. At least the water was crystal clear, so she could see any critters that might be waiting to eat her. Sweat trickled down her temple. She wiped it away with her arm, careful not to impede her view.

The woman still stood in the same spot, staring at something on the far side of the river.

Gia scanned the opposite shore but couldn't see anything of interest, so she resumed walking toward her.

"Gia, stop." Trevor had pulled the kayaks farther up onto the shore and laid the paddles across the seat compartment. He started to follow her. "You have to stop."

She pointed toward the woman and looked back at him, willing him to understand.

Trevor craned his neck to see past her, then drew his eyebrows together and shook his head.

Gia turned back around just in time to see the very top of the woman's stick disappear into the forest along with the back of her cape, and then she was gone.

Gia hurried to reach the spot the woman had just vacated, then spared a quick glance across the river. Whatever had held the woman's gaze was either gone or Gia couldn't see it. She gave up, turned around, and caught sight of the woman moving through the brush at a slow but steady pace. She started after her.

"Gia, this isn't safe." Trevor had almost caught up.

Surely it couldn't be too dangerous if an older woman who relied on a stick to walk was navigating the path so easily. There was probably a trail just into the brush.

Gia hurried as quickly as she could, but pricker bushes caught at her, scratching her bare legs. Thankfully, she'd worn sneakers with her shorts instead of sandals. Of course, they were probably ruined after her plunge into the river. Maybe she should just give up and turn back. She could always let Leo, or Hunt if she ever heard from him again, know where she'd seen the woman, and let them come back and search for her.

But if the woman disappeared, Gia might never find her again. Did it really matter? There was no way for Hayes to pin Marcia's murder on her. Did his opinion matter that much? No. She stopped and looked around. She'd been so focused on catching the woman she hadn't noticed her surroundings. She stood in the middle of the thick forest. No trail was visible.

If not for the sounds of Trevor bumbling through the thicket behind her, she'd have thought she was the only person around for miles. Her and the woman she'd lost sight of.

A black blur through the trees not far ahead propelled her forward. Hopefully, it was the woman and not a bear. If she couldn't catch her this time, she'd head back, but she had to give it one more shot. What if the woman had witnessed Marcia's murder?

Gia stumbled out of the forest into a clearing. The woman stood at the far end, holding her stick, staring straight at Gia.

Or what if the woman had killed Marcia?

Chapter 16

"What do you want?" the woman yelled across the clearing. It was the same gravelly voice Gia remembered from the trail. The woman stood stiff, clutching her stick tightly with both hands.

"I'm sorry. I didn't mean to frighten you." Gia held her hands up in front of her in a gesture of surrender. She'd probably scared the poor woman half to death chasing after her in the middle of the forest. "I just wanted to ask you a few questions. Do you remember me?"

The woman shook her head.

"We met on the trail last week. I had my dog with me, and you offered me a piece of advice."

The woman tilted her head, but her expression remained hidden in the shadows beneath her hood. "A big, black dog."

"Yes."

"Beautiful animal." The woman took a few steps closer. "With intelligent eyes and a kind soul."

"Yup. That's Thor."

Trevor stumbled out of the woods at Gia's side and plowed into her, almost knocking both of them down. "Are you crazy? What were you think—"

"I'm sorry, Trevor. I needed to speak to someone."

Trevor studied the woman as if he hadn't noticed her before. "I'm sorry."

"It's okay." Gia moved forward slowly, careful not to spook the woman, and closed the gap between them.

Trevor kept pace at her side.

When she reached the woman, she held out a hand. "I'm Gia Morelli. It's a pleasure to meet you."

After glancing back and forth between the two of them, the woman finally took her hand. "Cybil Devane."

Gia gestured toward Trevor. "And this is my friend, Trevor Barnes."

"Nice to meet you, Trevor." She took his hand and held it. "Such contentment. You are one who is truly at peace."

Trevor smiled. "I am indeed."

"This one, on the other hand." She released his hand, pointed toward Gia, and narrowed her eyes. "Last time I saw you, you seemed very conflicted. This time, not quite as much. Did you take my advice?"

"Actually, I wasn't sure if you were speaking figuratively or literally."

"Well, you certainly were headed down the less traveled trail in the forest, but I was referring to your state of mind at the time." The woman pulled her cloak tighter around her. "You seemed conflicted, your expression troubled. It just hit me, as it sometimes does, that you were making the wrong choice."

Gia was pretty sure she'd been thinking of heading back to New York at the time the woman had stopped her. Lately, she'd been thinking more and more of staying in Florida. "And now? Do I still seem conflicted?"

Cybil shifted the hood of her cloak back a bit, revealing her bright blue eyes and thick black hair interspersed with strands of white. She stared hard at Gia for a moment. "You seem less conflicted. More in control. I think you are maybe headed in the right direction now."

Maybe staying and fighting for her café was the right decision. Maybe she'd even win the fight. "Can you see how things will turn out?"

"Oh, dear, no." Cybil laughed, a wonderful sound, like wind chimes tinkling. "I'm not a prophet, just sometimes get impressions based on what I see in someone's expression. No psychic talent, I'm afraid, just keen powers of observation."

Gia laughed. She liked Cybil. The thought of her having any involvement in Marcia's murder seemed unlikely. But she pressed on. "Did you happen to see anyone else in the woods that day?"

"I'm sure I saw a lot of people."

Gia studied the walking stick. It seemed to be the same one she'd seen her with last time. It reached above her head, seemed to be made from a large branch. It didn't appear to have any bloodstains. "The woman I'm asking about was found dead a little while after I ran into you."

Her hand flew to her chest. "Oh my."

"Her name was Marcia Steers."

Cybil shook her head. "Doesn't ring any bells."

"She was wearing a hot pink sundress and high-heeled, leopard print sandals."

"Oh goodness. She certainly would have stood out hiking through the forest in a getup like that."

"But you don't remember seeing her?"

"I'm sorry, dear, but no."

Gia forced a smile as the one good lead she'd thought she had fizzled and died. "Thank you, Cybil."

"Of course, dear. I'm sorry I couldn't be more help."

"Thank you for taking the time to speak with me." She smiled. "And for the advice. It helped a lot."

"You're very welcome." She started to turn away, then stopped and turned back to Gia, deep furrows marring her brow. "The only other person I recall seeing in the woods that day was that police officer."

"Police officer?"

"Yes. I've seen him around town before. Tall fellow. Dark hair."

Captain Hayes had dark hair. Then again, so did Hunt. But what would Hunt have been doing in the forest? Captain Hayes, on the other hand, had shown up almost immediately after the 911 call had been made and had admitted to camping nearby with his son. "What was the officer doing when you saw him?"

She closed her eyes and frowned as if trying to remember. "Seemed as if he were looking for something. Just kind of wandering through the woods, looking around, occasionally glancing back over his shoulder."

"Was he on the trail?"

"No, I saw him earlier, before I started out on the trail." She opened her eyes. "I'm sorry, but that's all I remember."

"Thank you. That helps a lot. Can I ask you something, though?"

"Why stop now?" Mischief danced in Cybil's eyes.

Gia grinned. "Do you often hike through the woods not on trails?"

"All the time."

"Isn't it dangerous?"

"I've been hiking these here woods since I was a child. Besides, what's life without a little danger?" She winked. "Keeps things interesting."

Gia thanked her again, sorry to have nothing more to ask. The woman had spunk, and Gia had a feeling she had tons of interesting stories to share.

"Y'all be careful heading back to the river now." She looked up at the blue sky and squinted, then raised a hand to shield her eyes from the sun. "Storms'll be comin' soon."

"Storms? It's beautiful out."

"They're comin'. Bad ones tonight, I reckon. Time to head back." She said the last bit quietly, as if to herself. "I'll see you again soon."

Gia thought about asking her to go to the police station to issue a statement, but what had she really seen? It hardly seemed worth inconveniencing her. Besides, now that she knew her name, Hunt, if he ever showed up again, or Leo could probably find her if they needed her. If Cybil Devane was her real name. "How will I find you?"

"You won't, but we'll happen upon each other again." She took Gia's hand in both of hers. "Some paths are meant to cross, my dear. Maybe next time we'll chat for a while."

"I'd like that." Gia squeezed her hand, then let go and watched the woman shamble across the clearing.

At least Trevor had witnessed the conversation. If nothing else, he could corroborate the fact Cybil was real and not a figment of Gia's imagination or a fabricated alibi. She looked up at the sky. "How long do you think before it rains?"

Trevor, who'd remained quiet until then, shielded his eyes and looked around at the sky. "Don't know. I heard the storms were coming in later today."

"Still no word on Harley?" Gia hoped he'd find somewhere safe to stay or take her up on her offer to use the apartment if they got storms, but she doubted he would. Harley had been wandering the streets of Boggy Creek a lot longer than Gia had lived there.

"No. Nothing. No one's seen him, but it's not the first time he's disappeared for a while."

"All right." There wasn't really anything she could do, so she'd just keep leaving him food and papers and hope he'd come back around. She'd have to remember to mention it to Hunt if she ever heard from him again. Maybe he could check around. "Do you think we have time to finish kayaking?"

A wide smile spread across Trevor's face. "You bet we do."

They made it back to the kayaks without incident, moving a little more carefully than they had going in, and Trevor pushed Gia's kayak off the shore and into the water. He held it parallel to the shore for her to climb in.

She put one foot in, then stopped. Scratches crisscrossed her leg, probably from the prickers that had been grabbing at her when she'd run into the brush. A small black bug crawled up her leg, and she flicked it off. Then she saw another. She swatted that one, but it still clung to her ankle just above her sock. "What are these things?"

"Ticks." Trevor reached past her and plucked it off, then threw it into the water. "Stand up and get them off."

"Them?" She yanked her foot out of the kayak and stood on the shore scanning her legs for more of the creepy little creatures.

Trevor brushed the back of her leg. "You're going to have to check yourself when you get home later. If you find any, just pull them out and put them in a plastic bag with some rubbing alcohol."

"What? Why?"

"Only way to kill them." He brushed at his own leg where two ticks crawled slowly up his calf.

"What do you mean pull them out?"

"When they reach a spot they like, usually where something impedes their forward motion, like a waistband, or they reach your head, they stop and attach themselves."

Gia's stomach flipped over. "Attach?"

"Yes." Trevor pulled a tick off his arm. "They stick their heads in and suck your blood until they are fully engorged before falling off. But they can carry diseases, so you want to be careful to get them out right away."

She searched her legs, frantic to get any of the bloodsucking little vampires off her.

"Some of them are smaller than a pinhead, so you have to search really well, especially in your hair. Scrape your nails through every inch of scalp and make sure nothing catches."

"Can't I just get in the shower?"

"Well, yeah, but water doesn't kill them." He finally looked up at her and held up a finger. "Oh, and put your clothes in the dryer as soon as you walk in. Water won't kill ticks, but the heat will kill any that remain in your clothes. Luckily, you have on shorts. Would have been worse with pants. Might not have noticed them."

Though she didn't see any more ticks, the sensation of things crawling on her remained as she climbed into the kayak. She squirmed, and the boat rocked. "Couldn't you have warned me about those things?"

"I would have, if you hadn't run off half-cocked through the forest."

She held on to his wrist before he could let go. "I'm sorry, Trevor. I wouldn't have run after her if it wasn't important."

"I figured as much from the conversation." He patted her hand, then stood. "Come on. If we hurry, we might still be able to see the manatees before we have to head back."

"Manatees?"

"Yup, you'll love 'em." Trevor climbed into his kayak and pushed off.

Gia followed, her kayak rocking as she tried to find her rhythm again.

In the seemingly serene water a few feet from where they'd left the kayaks, a turtle swam. In a swirl of water, a small, half-submerged alligator Gia hadn't noticed whirled and grabbed it faster than she would have thought possible, then disappeared beneath the surface.

Chapter 17

Gia started to towel her hair dry after her shower, then cringed at the pain in her shoulders. As much as she'd loved kayaking, especially seeing the manatees as Trevor had promised, the experience had left her sore in muscles she didn't even know existed. Never mind the hair dryer. She hung the towel over the rack to dry, then headed for the kitchen. Her hair could dry on its own.

She fed Thor, then checked the yard thoroughly for snakes and other critters, before letting him out into the fenced area beside the deck and watching him until he was done. Once she had him back in the house with the door firmly locked behind him, she took a glass dish of lasagna Savannah had made from the freezer and popped it into the microwave and poured a cup of tea. She'd planned on spending the evening relaxing, maybe reading a few chapters of her book, but her conversation with Cybil had left her with no clue about Marcia's killer. She'd been disappointed Cybil hadn't been able to offer any kind of leads.

She let Thor back in and took her tea to the living room, then placed it on a coaster on the coffee table. She went back to the bedroom and got her laptop and set it on the table beside the tea. As soon as dinner was ready, she'd do some research. No sense letting the evening go to waste when she could put the time to use looking up the names from the list.

She grabbed a toy for Thor and filled it with peanut butter. A small niggle of guilt tugged at her that she hadn't taken him out to play all day, but thick, black clouds hovered overhead, and she worried about lightning. "Here you go, boy."

Thor took the treat and trotted into the living room. He knew the routine.

When the microwave beeped, she took her lasagna to the living room and settled on the couch with Thor at her feet between the couch and coffee table. "Don't you snatch any of my dinner, you hear me, mister? All that kayaking made me hungry."

She took a bite and opened her computer, then typed *"Sean McNeil"* into the search box, hit enter, and took another bite, grateful Savannah had sent her home with leftovers the other night when Gia had gone for dinner with Savannah and Joey.

Gia scrolled past the first couple of pages of social media sites. She didn't know enough about Sean to find him, and the name Sean McNeil proved to be more common than she'd hoped. She'd reached the fourth page of Sean McNeils before she finally found something of interest, the headline, *Bar Owner Fined in Student's Death.*

She clicked on the local paper's website and pulled up the article dated twenty-two years earlier, then stuffed a forkful of pasta and cheese with a crumble of spicy sausage into her mouth. Mmm... Savannah sure could cook Italian food. If Gia ever decided to add dinner to her café menu, she knew whom to hit up for recipes.

She skimmed the article while she finished off her lasagna. Seemed a twenty-one-year-old student had been clearly inebriated when he'd walked into McNeil's with a few friends. According to witnesses, Sean served him a shot and a beer; then the victim had stumbled out of the bar and into the street where he was struck and killed by an oncoming vehicle. Tragic, but the driver was not indicted as the incident was ruled an accident.

Sean, however, was fined ten thousand dollars for overserving the student, Frederick Masters. An update at the bottom of the article dated two years later stated though the fine had been paid, McNeil's had never recovered from the tragedy and had closed two years after the incident. Right around the same time everyone seemed to take an interest in the zoning information on the bar. Just after Sara Mills was murdered.

She brought the search engine back up and typed in *"Frederick Masters."* The only thing she could find was an obituary. Not surprising considering household computers weren't as common twenty-two years ago. The obituary was a short blurb in the back of the local paper stating that Frederick Masters was an honor student studying engineering and had been a local high school football star before moving on to play college ball. His death had been ruled an accident. He was survived by his father, Floyd. *Bingo.* She'd found the connection, but what to do with it? Also survived by a brother, Dion. The date and times of the services were listed as well as a plea for charitable donations in lieu of flowers by Frederick's aunt, Carolyn Masters.

She looked up Carolyn Masters and found another obituary. This one for a Carolyn Masters Hayes of Boggy Creek dated a few years ago, survived by her son, Howard, and her brother, Floyd. She couldn't find anything about a Dion Masters.

She typed *"Floyd Masters"* into the box and waited. Nothing happened. She sipped her tea and waited for the search to load. Sometimes internet could be slow in Rolling Pines.

A nagging itch on the outside of her ankle started up again, and she pulled up her pajama pant leg. An angry red spot with a dark dot in its center sat just where the band of her sock had lain. She tried to see it closer, but couldn't tell what the black spot was.

She grabbed her cell phone, then stood with her foot propped awkwardly on the couch, opened the camera, and zoomed in on the spot. Between the angle and the size of the spot, she still couldn't make out what it was, even fully magnified. She snapped a picture, then sat and opened it. She magnified it until the black dot came into focus. Sure enough, the tiny speck sticking up out of her ankle had creepy little legs attached.

Ah jeez. How was she going to get a hold of something that small?

She dialed Savannah's number.

"Hello?"

"Savannah?"

"Gia? Are you okay? You sound a little frazzled."

"I have a tick."

A moment's hesitation followed before Savannah finally said, "So pull it out."

"No. I mean, I can't. It's too small. I can't get a grip on it, and it's stuck in my ankle. It looks like its head is in there."

"Use tweezers."

Ugh… Why hadn't she thought of that?

An alarm sounded on her phone. Odd, she didn't remember setting an alarm, and as far as she could remember, she didn't have any plans for the evening. "Hang on a minute, Savannah. An alarm is going off on my phone."

She pulled the phone away from her ear and read the urgent weather alert. A line of strong storms capable of producing tornadoes moving through the area. A tornado watch was in effect.

"Tornadoes?"

"Oh, yeah. I saw that on TV earlier. Do you know what to do if there's a tornado?"

Fill the car with gas, point it north, and head back to New York. "I haven't the slightest clue."

"Go into an interior room, or in your case, the hallway, since all of your rooms have windows."

"Oh. Lucky me."

"Are you okay, Gia?"

"Gee, I don't know, Savannah. So far today I've had a poisonous snake on my deck, seen an alligator eat a poor, unsuspecting turtle, gotten a tick, and now I'm sitting smack in the middle of a tornado watch. Not to mention last week's fire or the tinderbox I'm living in out here with no escape route. When you were busy spouting all those ridiculous statistics regarding the lack of crime in the neighborhood, you failed to mention the place was a death trap." Winded, Gia took a moment to catch her breath.

"Done?"

"Not even close. Just trying not to hyperventilate."

"While you regain control of yourself, it's my turn to talk. Granted, you're going to come across snakes, both venomous and not. It's Florida, Gia. Snakes live here. Actually, snakes live in most places, even in New York. For the most part, they are just as afraid of you as you are of them."

"Somehow I don't think that's true."

"Well, trust me, it is. It's not like you're Indiana Jones descending into a pit full of asps, for crying out loud. And as for the alligator, what would you have him eat? A nice salad perhaps?"

"Sarcasm isn't helping anything."

"Neither is freaking out."

"I'm not freaking out, I'm just…" She took a deep breath and let it out slowly. Okay, maybe she was freaking out. A little. But she didn't have to admit it out loud.

"Do you remember that time I went out to Fire Island with the other dancers from my show? You didn't come because you had to work."

"I remember." *Though I don't know what it has to do with anything.*

"I found three ticks crawling on me that day."

"You never told me that."

"Because there was nothing to tell. A bug crawled on me, so I brushed it off and went about my day."

"When you say it like that—"

"There is no other way to say it. And as for the tornadoes, I have to admit, I'm a little freaked out about them too. I'm not a huge fan, but we don't get them often, and when we do, they're usually not very strong."

Gia got up and headed to the bathroom for tweezers. "Well, when you say it that way..."

"I didn't say it any way." She laughed. "I just put things in perspective to keep you from having some sort of an episode."

Gia sighed. What could she say? Savannah wasn't wrong.

"You're right about the fire. The situation up there is a little scary, but that's why you are going before the board tomorrow night to discuss the possibility of adding a fire exit."

"True."

"No matter where you live, there are going to be downsides. And you want to talk about death traps? Those soaring apartment buildings y'all live in up there in New York make Rolling Pines look like it's right off a fire safety poster."

"I wouldn't go that far." But Savannah wasn't completely wrong either. "I understand what you're saying, Savannah."

"If you are looking for excuses to run back home, it's not necessary, Gia. You are a big girl, and you have every right to decide where you want to live. As far as everything else, if there's something within your control, by all means, fix it. If not, you just have to deal with it."

Gia squeezed the tick gently between the tweezers and pulled. She'd need her phone to magnify the tip of the tweezers to see if she'd gotten it. "Hold on a minute, Savannah."

"Sure."

She hovered the phone over the tip of the tweezers. Sure enough, a tiny tick. She dropped it into the plastic bag full of alcohol with the two bigger ones she'd taken off before she'd gotten in the shower. "All right, I'm back."

Savannah sighed. "I'm sorry, Gia. I shouldn't have jumped down your throat."

"No, you're right. I do have to get a grip. It's just a lot to get used to. There are a lot of things I love about Florida too." She thought of the lush forest she'd witnessed while kayaking. "I also saw monkeys and manatees today. And they were amazing."

"Yes, they are."

"Are you okay, Savannah? Lately you seem... I don't know..." The term Cybil had used jumped into her head. "Conflicted."

"I have a lot on my mind."

"Anything you want to talk about?"

"Hunt, for one. I haven't heard from him in days, have you?"

"No." She couldn't blame her for being worried about Hunt. They had always been very close, and he was acting more than a little strange lately. "But Leo said he was out of town following up on a lead."

"He told me the same thing. Grudgingly."

Gia examined her entire ankle. Nothing. "Did he mention a second body when you spoke to him?"

"No. Why, is there another body?"

"I'm not sure. When he told me Hunt went out of town to follow up on a lead, he slipped and said it had something to do with a second body. When I tried to get him to elaborate, he clammed right up."

"He didn't mention anything to me about another body at all," Savannah said.

"Is that unusual? That he would keep something from you?" Gia pulled up her pajama pant leg and studied her other ankle. No more ticks. At least, not that she could see.

"That man has been an open book since we were kids. He'd share anything with me. And yet, suddenly, his lips are sealed up tight, won't say boo about Hunt or Marcia's case. A case that obviously has something to do with my mother's death."

"Is that what's bugging you?"

"Among other things."

"Can I do anything to help?"

Silence hummed over the line.

Gia waited, giving Savannah time to figure out what she might need. She smoothed antibiotic ointment onto the tick bite and hoped the itching would stop before she clawed off half her skin. Leaving the ointment on the counter, since she figured she'd probably need it again before the night was over, she headed for the living room.

When Savannah finally spoke, her voice came over the line so low Gia had to strain to hear her. "I need this case to be solved, and I need to know how it involved my mother. Because she *is* involved. Somehow. I can't prove it, but I know in my gut this has something to do with her."

"I agree."

"You do?" She seemed surprised Gia had come to the same conclusion.

"Yes."

"Then you'll help me?"

"Help you what?"

"Solve the case."

"Uh..." *I didn't say that.*

Savannah was her best friend, like a sister, and she'd been there for Gia through everything, never losing faith in her for even a second. Hers had been the only support that had never faltered.

"Of course, I'll help you."

Thunder rumbled, rattling the glasses in her china cabinet. "Did you hear that?"

"The thunder?"

"Yeah. Are you having storms there?"

"Yes. Pretty bad ones."

Gia used the remote to turn on the TV, then switched to the local news station. A severe weather alert scrolled across the bottom of the screen.

Thunder boomed again, louder this time.

"If you live on the following roads, take cover now. There's rotation overhead." A harried-looking meteorologist rattled off a list of familiar-sounding roads. "Palmetto Trail..."

I live on Palmetto Trail. "What does rotation overhead mean?"

"Where'd you hear that?" Savannah sounded alert in a way she hadn't before, all signs of the depression that seemed to be weighing on her gone.

"The weather guy just said if you live on Palmetto Trail, take cover."

Thunder rattled the windows. The electricity went out, plunging the house into darkness. "Savannah?"

Thor lurched to his feet and barked.

"Gia, are you all right? Go into the hallway, now. Take Thor."

Gia stood in the middle of the living room and stared out the window. Rain pounded against the house. Lightning flashed, bolt after bolt, illuminating the yard. Mesmerizing. The tall, thin palm tree outside her front window bent in half.

Her phone sounded three beeps, then dropped the call.

"Come, Thor." She started around the couch toward the hallway.

Lightning flashed again, illuminating a figure running full speed across her yard toward the house.

Gia froze. Someone was out there.

With the next flash, the figure was gone.

Rain pounded harder. She hadn't thought it was possible to rain any harder.

She grabbed Thor's collar and ran for the hallway, leaned her back against the wall, and slid down to sit.

Something banged against the front of the house.

Thor barked wildly.

She covered her head with her hands, leaning against Thor, trying to keep him against the wall.

The banging came again, louder, drowning out the sound of the rain.

Thor squirmed out from between Gia and the wall and bolted toward the front of the house.

Chapter 18

Gia ran after Thor. "Thor, no!"

He leaped against the front door, frantically scratching at the wood with his front paws, jumping off the floor, up and down, on his back paws.

"Thor, no. It's just a storm." She grabbed his collar and tried to soothe him, petting his head calmly, despite her wildly shaking hands. *Less conflicted my ass. Cybil should see me now.*

Three loud knocks rattled the door.

"Gia!" A man's voice screamed through the door. "Open up. It's Hunt."

Gia wrapped an arm around Thor's neck to keep him from running out into the storm, and whipped the door open.

Hunt blocked the open doorway as he staggered inside and slammed the door behind him. He leaned his back against the door.

Though she couldn't see anything, there was no mistaking the sound of water dripping all over her tile floor.

"I'm sorry," Hunt wheezed.

Gia still held Thor to keep him from jumping on Hunt.

Lightning flashed again, backlighting Hunt, offering a silhouette view of his slouched body. He cradled his ribs and inhaled a shallow breath. "I'm sorry."

"Sorry for what?"

"Scaring you." He petted Thor's head. "And Thor. Twice in one week."

"I thought there was a tornado out there."

"There's more than one tornado out there tonight." Struggling to control his breathing, Hunt ushered Gia and Thor back into the hallway, then pulled Gia down with him and sat with his back against the wall. He tucked her beneath his arm and pulled her close. "Down, Thor."

Thor lapped up some of the water dripping from Hunt's clothes, then sat in front of them and lay down, resting his head in Gia's lap.

"Good boy, Thor." She stroked the soft fur on his head, the action soothing her as much as she hoped it was soothing him. "Savannah must be worried sick. I was on the phone with her when I lost service."

"I sent Leo over to the house. He knew I was coming out here."

Gia shifted to face him, even though she couldn't see more than a silhouette in the darkness. "What are you doing here, anyway?"

"Leo told me about the phone you dropped off, so I wanted to get out here and have a look around before the storms hit."

"And?"

"I was too late."

"No kidding." She ran her hand over his arm. "You're soaking wet."

"Your powers of observation astound me. You should have been a detective."

She thought about Savannah's request to help her solve Marcia's case. "Maybe."

"Just stay away from this case, Miss Detective." He yanked his wet shirt over his head and tossed it aside. "I'm serious, Gia. The fire investigator got in touch earlier. He said the preliminary reports indicate a cigarette started the fire. They found a small pile of them in the woods on that side of the house."

"How would they get there?"

"Obviously, someone was out there smoking," he said.

"Yeah, but why would someone be standing and smoking in the woods by my house?"

He stared at her. "Why do you think, Detective Morelli?"

No need to be sarcastic, Detective Tall, Dark, and Annoying. "I have no idea. I assume someone was watching the house for some reason?"

"I can't say for sure, but that's the general consensus."

Gia racked her brain. "I don't remember ever seeing Maybelle smoke."

"Me neither, but that doesn't rule her out."

"No. I think Hank smokes."

Hunt nodded. "He does."

"Do you think he killed Marcia?"

Hunt was quiet for a few minutes, seemingly contemplating his answer.

Gia stood and felt her way along the hallway to the linen closet and grabbed a couple of towels. She handed one to Hunt to dry himself off and used the other to mop up the water he'd dripped on the floor.

"We have reason to believe the killer was right handed." He rubbed the right side of his jaw. "Hank is left handed."

She tossed the towels aside and sat back down. "Why did you two get into a fight, anyway? You never said."

"I had questions he didn't want to answer." He shifted position, either to get more comfortable or to avoid answering her questions.

She wasn't sure which, although she had her suspicions.

"That's enough talk about the case for now." He pulled her closer again. "May as well relax. We're going to be here for a little while."

Gia snuggled back against him and inhaled deeply. Being cocooned in his embrace, surrounded by the woodsy scent of his aftershave, made her feel safe. "So what now?"

"Now we wait for these storms to end."

"Are they always this bad?" Gia scratched the tick bite on her leg, which had begun to itch again in earnest.

"No. This is unusual. I was headed here from Tampa, and I saw a tractor trailer get thrown right across the highway."

A chill raced through her. "Was anyone hurt?"

"I don't know. I was on an overpass when I saw it below me. No way for me to get to it, but people did stop, including a police cruiser."

Gia scratched her head, the feeling of things crawling on her in the dark driving her almost crazy enough to get up and brave the storm. She lurched away from him, stood, and brushed at her clothes. Even Hunt's embrace couldn't keep her still while things could be crawling all over her.

Hunt stood and grabbed her wrists. "Are you okay?"

"I found a bunch of ticks on me today, and now I keep feeling like things are crawling all over me." Ticks just went on her admittedly irrational phobia of spiders list.

"Come here." He pulled her back down to sit with him. "Did you check yourself good?"

"Yes. I took one out of my leg right before the storm hit."

"Did you check your head?"

"As well as I could." She ran her fingers over her scalp again.

"Come here." He sat up straighter, took out his phone, and lit the flashlight, then guided her to lay her head in his lap. "Relax, Gia."

She did as instructed. At least, she tried.

Hunt separated strands of hair and started to search her head. His nails scraped gently against her scalp. His fingers weaved between strands of hair.

Gia's eyes drifted shut, and she focused on the feel of his warm fingers against her head, his gentle touch soothing her.

As he finished each side of her head, he coaxed her into a new position and continued his search. His fingers brushed against her neck, lifted the strands away, baring her skin to the cool air. Finally, he rolled her onto her back so she was lying with her head in his lap, staring up at him. He set the phone aside, leaving the light facing up. "Nothing there."

"Thank you."

"You're welcome." He continued to slide his fingers through her hair. "Do you feel any better now?"

"Yes." *But I'd feel much better if you never stop doing that.* She made no move to sit up.

Hunt made no move to stop.

"Were you seeing her, Hunt?" She closed her eyes and held her breath. She cared for Hunt, wanted something more with him than friendship, or even family. But she couldn't share anything with a man she didn't trust, and if he'd kept the fact he was seeing someone from her while he continued to hang out with her, she'd view that as lying. Or at least being deceptive.

"If I answer that question honestly, will you trust me?"

Would she? "I guess that depends on your answer."

"I'll tell you what, you ask me whatever you want to know, and I'll answer the questions I can, and be honest about why I can't answer the others. Fair enough?"

She started to sit up, but he guided her back down.

She went willingly. For now. "Were you seeing Marcia?" She held her breath waiting for his answer.

"I was…."

She jerked up.

"Relax, Gia, lie back down. I like being here with you like this. It relaxes me. Please." His voice had turned husky, filled with emotion.

She did as he asked, staring up at him in the light cast by the flashlight beam.

"I was seeing Marcia—at one time. When I am dating a woman, even if it's a casual relationship and we both know we're not going to get married and live happily ever after, I don't see anyone else. And I insist on the same respect in return. Marcia knew that. Our relationship wasn't serious. Neither of us expected to have a future together, but we enjoyed each other's company. For a while."

He stopped for a moment and took a few deep breaths. "All Marcia had to do was be honest with me and tell me she'd met someone else, wanted to move on. It would have been fine, and we'd have parted friends. Instead, she snuck around behind my back. I found out at the Fourth of July picnic and blew up. Not because she'd found someone else, but because she'd used me and betrayed my trust."

She waited, but he didn't elaborate. "Used you in what way?"

"She was dating a married man, had been for a while, but kept me around so his wife wouldn't become suspicious."

"How did you find all of that out?"

"A mutual friend."

Apparently more his friend than hers.

"I didn't know whom she was seeing, just that he was local and married. So we parted ways, and that was that. If we saw each other around town, we shared a courteous hello and kept walking. Until a few weeks ago." He cradled Gia's head between his hands and lifted it to kiss her forehead, then sat up straighter, his posture stiff.

Though disappointed to lose the contact, Gia sat beside him and studied his profile among the shadows cast by the phone's light.

"Marcia wasn't a bad person. She just made some bad choices, and apparently the guilt had eaten away at her for years. She knew you and I were friends, or maybe something more, so she came to me." He pulled his knees up and rested his elbows on his bent knees, then looked down and clasped his hands behind his head. "She was so scared. Didn't know where to turn. But she came to me. She said she knew I'd help her even though things between us had ended badly, because that's the kind of man I am. Except she was wrong, because despite my best efforts, I couldn't protect her."

He rubbed his hands over his face.

"Why did she need protection?"

"That's just it. We weren't sure. She kept catching glimpses of a man she thought might be following her, but she wasn't sure why."

"Did it have anything to do with the information she was trying to get to me?"

"I don't know. Marcia had been staying with me for a few weeks, not in any sort of romantic way, but because she was terrified to go home, but she was still secretive. I think it was just her way. Then she called and said she was leaving town with her lover. He'd decided to leave his wife and run off with her. She just needed to meet with someone first and she was gone." He shook his head. "She didn't tell me it was you."

"If Marcia was staying with you, whose breakfast was still on her table? No way that food was sitting there for a week. A day or two at most."

His breathing grew more ragged. "I have no idea. Maybe she went home for something first and decided to have something to eat. She was going back and forth occasionally, picking up clothing and stuff. Or maybe someone else was at the house."

"The note she left me makes more sense now that I know she wasn't staying there. I couldn't figure out why she'd tell me to just go in."

"She didn't tell me much of what was going on," Hunt said.

"Did she tell you anything?"

"A little, and I was investigating, but she got impatient when Maybelle found out she was seeing Hank."

"I thought Maybelle found out *after* Marcia was killed?" At least that's how Maybelle had made it sound, though Gia had her suspicions she'd already known. Maybelle as a suspect became much more believable in light of Hunt's new information. If her husband had told her he was leaving, she could have gone off the deep end.

"No. Marcia still didn't tell me who she was dating, just that his wife had found out and threatened her. Maybe that's why they decided to run off together. Who knows?"

"You know what? When Maybelle accused me of trying to steal her husband, she said I'd need someone to support me once the café went under, as if it never occurred to her that I'd do something else to support myself." Considering how lazy Maybelle was, that wasn't too surprising. "Maybe she was worried about how she'd support herself if he took off, and decided if she got rid of his mistress, he'd stay with her."

"It's possible, but so is anything else at this point. I just wish Marcia had been more forthcoming with information."

"Wouldn't it have been easier for you to investigate if you'd known what was going on?"

"Yup. But she wasn't a trusting woman. Anyway, the day she was killed, she called me, asked me to meet her at the forest recreation area where we used to hike. She said she had documents she was trying to get to someone, but she couldn't wait around any longer, and she was afraid to leave anything at the house when she took off, so she was going to give me everything and let me decide how to handle it." A tear glistened on his cheek, and he swiped it away.

"There was a spot we used to go up there, a small clearing we'd sometimes pack a picnic lunch and go to eat. I waited there, but she never showed. I was still waiting when the call came in about a body found in the forest." He lowered his head into his hands. "I knew it would turn out to be her."

Gia put a hand on his shoulder and squeezed. "I'm sorry, Hunt."

He sat up. "Marcia begged me not to tell you she was staying with me, but I couldn't continue pursuing any sort of relationship with you without being honest. That's why I backed off."

"I understand. Thank you for telling me the truth."

He nodded and pulled her back against him, then wrapped his arms around her.

Thor snuggled closer to them.

The storm raged, pummeling the house.

"So, now what?" Gia asked.

"First, I finish investigating, then I try to get my badge back."

"Will you be able to get back on the force?"

"I think so. I hope so. Either way, I have to see this through first."

"Where were you for the past week? Leo said you were following up a lead about a second body."

"Leo has a big mouth."

Gia laughed. "That may be true, but in his defense, it slipped out by accident."

"I left town to follow a couple of leads, but they didn't go where I expected."

"Can you tell me what they were?"

"If I do, can you promise to stay out of this investigation?"

Major dilemma. She couldn't lie to him, especially not after he'd been so honest with her. But at the same time, she couldn't betray Savannah's trust either.

"That's what I figured." He didn't sound angry, just resigned.

"I'm sorry, Hunt, I—"

"It's okay. I appreciate you being honest with me." He lifted her off him and slid around to face her. "That's all I ask, Gia. I have feelings for you, feelings that confuse me because I've never felt this way about anyone else. You're like family, and yet not. You're more. And I'd like to see where this will lead. The only thing I ask is that there are no lies between us. Ever. Trust and respect are very important to me. I'll always understand if you can't tell me something, and I'll never pry." He grinned. "Not too much anyway. But we always have to be honest with one another."

He leaned toward her, then lowered his lips to hers. Hesitant at first, gentle, but then he pulled her closer, deepened the kiss.

A cell phone rang.

Hunt pulled away, kissed her once more, a quick peck, then answered his phone.

Gia started to stand, but he weaved his fingers between hers and held her hand.

"Okay. I'm at Gia's…. She's fine. Are you with Savannah? Let her know Gia's fine, she just lost cell phone service…thanks." Hunt disconnected the call, stood, and stuffed his phone into his pocket. "I have to go."

"Is something wrong?"

"The storms are bad, Gia, really bad. And there are a lot of people in trouble. Badge or not, I have to help. I'll be back as soon as I can."

"Okay." She kissed him and tore herself away so she didn't cling and beg him to stay where he'd be safe. "Be careful."

"Always."

Chapter 19

Gia unlocked the café door and hit the switch, breathing a sigh of relief when the lights came on. Electricity had still not been restored to Rolling Pines when she'd left, so she'd packed an overnight bag and hoped for the best. If everything worked in town, she'd spend the night at the apartment.

She locked the door behind her and turned on all the lights in the dining room, then dropped her overnight bag onto a chair in the corner of her office. She set her laptop on her desk. Sometime today she wanted to finish her search of Floyd Masters, then see what she could find out about his nephew, good ole Captain Hayes.

Before starting her prep for the day, she took a quick peek out the back door. Not only was Harley's dinner gone, the table and chair she'd left out there for him had disappeared as well. The newspapers scattered across the parking lot and caught up in the trees and brush that had come down courtesy of last night's storms led her to believe Harley still hadn't returned. She'd have to go out later and clean up the mess. Great. Just what she needed, prolonged exposure to the back parking lot.

She grabbed an apron from a hook behind the door and pulled it over her head, tying it as she strode into the kitchen to start prepping. A quick inventory told her what she'd need, and she jotted everything down on a list and tacked it above the grill.

She first sliced a few thick slabs of ham on the slicer, then set them aside on a cutting board on the counter. She set out a bag of green peppers and a bag of onions. Once she finished washing and dicing everything for the western omelets, she filled bins and placed them in the refrigerator. Then she diced vegetables for omelets and lined those up in the fridge as well.

She set trays of bacon and sausage out on the grill and started the home fries.

"Hey there."

Gia jumped and pressed a hand against her chest.

"Sorry, I didn't mean to startle you." Savannah strode toward her.

"That's okay." Gia laughed. "I didn't hear you come in."

Savannah threw her arms around Gia and hugged her.

Confused, Gia hugged her back. "Is everything okay?"

Savannah stepped back, half laughing, half crying, and wiped her eyes. She sucked in a shaky breath. "I know it's probably silly, but I got so scared last night. When I lost your call, then heard on the news people had been killed in the storm, I felt sick until Leo was finally able to get through to Hunt. All I could think about was my last conversation with you, when I was a complete and total witch."

"What are you talking about?"

"When you were concerned about the ticks and I got nasty. I didn't mean it."

Gia smiled. "Of course, you did. I was acting like a baby, and you called me on it."

"Still… I could have been kinder."

"Sometimes you don't need to be coddled. Sometimes you need to be told to pull up your big girl pants and deal with reality. Which, come to think of it, I think you've actually said to me before." Gia laughed and squeezed Savannah's hand. "And only a truly close friend, your best friend, can get away with putting you in your place when the need arises. Thank you."

Savannah hugged her again. "You are my best friend, Gia, more of a sister really, but as much as I want you to stay here, I want you to be happy more."

"I know that. And I love you all the more for it. But I am happy here. I'm not gonna lie, it's an adjustment, and there are still things I have to get used to, and probably things I'll never get used to, but overall, I love it here. Boggy Creek is my home." The certainty surprised her. For the first time, she had no doubts about staying in Florida. "Accept it, you're stuck with me."

"Well, it sure took you long enough." Savannah winked and took a piece of bacon. "So, now that you're here to stay, what trouble can we get into?"

"Well, for starters, you can spray those pans and start filling them with home fries for the breakfast pies."

"Yes, ma'am." Savannah saluted and started lining up the pie tins.

Gia cracked eggs into a large glass bowl. "What were you saying about people getting killed in the storm?"

"So far, they've found eleven people dead."

They both paused a moment in silence, then made the sign of the cross. Not that Gia was particularly religious, but some things stuck from childhood, and it seemed appropriate to pray for those who'd lost their lives.

"Haven't you been watching the news?" Savannah asked.

"The electricity went out last night and never came back on, and I didn't even have cell phone service or internet." She hadn't realized how cut off she'd been from everything, including help. "I just got here, so I haven't had time to turn anything on."

Savannah wiped her hands on a paper towel, then went out into the dining room and turned on the TV in the corner and turned the volume way up. When she returned, she took the bins out of the fridge and started sprinkling the diced ham, peppers, and onions into the eggs Gia was scrambling. "A line of severe storms came through and spawned several large tornadoes. They think as many as ten or more tornadoes actually touched down. One of them just down the road from you, which is why they said there was rotation overhead."

While the thought scared her half to death, it didn't make her want to run home and pack. Progress. "I didn't realize how bad it was."

"There are still people missing and many more injured; homes were destroyed."

"Is there something we can do to help?"

"They're asking for donations. I'll head down later today with cases of water and whatever else I can donate."

"As soon as you hear what's needed let me know and I'll chip in too."

Someone knocked on the front door.

Gia glanced up at the clock. "Could you let Willow in, please, and have her put the chalkboard out front, but instead of the day's specials have her write, 'Storm victims, volunteers, and rescue workers eat free.'"

"Are you sure? You might end up giving away a lot of food."

"I'm sure. This is my home now, and it's the least I can do to help." Besides, she'd wanted to find a way to contribute something positive to the community, and now she could.

Savannah nodded and headed out to unlock the door.

"Oh, and do you know if they're opening a shelter?" Gia called after her.

Savannah stopped in the doorway. "They already opened the high school."

"Okay, could you call the bakery and ask if they can send over some extra rolls, then see if you can find out how many people are at the shelter, and we'll send over sandwiches."

Gia filled the tins Savannah had readied with the cooked western mixture and slid the breakfast pies into the oven. She lined up another set of tins and scrambled more eggs, then added crumbled bacon and sausage, diced ham, and onions for the meat lover's pies. She had to hurry and get the fillings cooked before she opened and needed the grill. Once she had them ready for the oven, she pulled more bacon and sausage from the freezer.

"Good morning." Willow's usual enthusiasm was missing, her eyes red-rimmed and swollen.

"Good morning. Is something wrong?"

"No, it's okay now." She waved it off and smiled, though tears still shimmered in her eyes. "When the storms hit"—she sniffled—"my mom was on her way home. She'd just called to say she was leaving work, but she never made it home. I had the news on and heard a tornado had touched down on the highway she takes home, and I was worried sick."

Gia put the food she was still holding on the counter and went to Willow. "Is she all right?"

Willow nodded. "She is, thank you. The highway was blocked with accidents, and she tried to go around, but a huge tree was blocking the entrance to our development. There's no other entrance, so she had to go to a friend's and wait out the storm, but she couldn't get ahold of me until this morning."

"Oh, honey." Gia hugged Willow. "Why are you here? You should be home with your mother."

"It's okay. She went with her friend to volunteer at the shelter, and I'd rather be here doing something than just sitting home watching the news."

"Well, there's plenty to do here. I'll be happy to keep you busy all day."

"Oh, right. That's actually what I came back here for. Frank from the bakery said he'd donate as many rolls as you need. He's making up more now, but he has no one to run them over yet. If it's okay, I'm going to pick them up."

"Sure, that'd be great, thank you."

"And I called my mom and told her you'd be sending sandwiches. They really appreciate it."

"Thanks, Willow."

"You bet."

Savannah stopped Willow on her way out. "Frank called back and said he'll send his son to help deliver the food later if you need help."

"Thanks." Willow seemed more herself when she left with a smile.

Savannah called to Gia from the doorway, "Earl wants to know if you have a minute."

She glanced at the clock. It was past the time she should have met him out front for a cup of coffee before she opened. "Of course. Could you start the bacon and sausage for me, and check the breakfast pies? Some of them should be about done."

"Sure." Savannah frowned. "Did you check if Harley took his dinner last night?"

"He didn't, and everything is all over the place back there. I'll have to get out there sometime later and clean up."

"Don't worry about it. I'll take care of it."

Relief rushed through her. "Thanks, Savannah."

"No problem. And I'll ask Leo to look around and see if he can find him."

"Thanks." Gia washed her hands, then headed out to the dining room. "Good morning, Earl. I'm sorry, I lost track of time."

"No sweat." He sat at his usual seat at the counter, a half-full cup of coffee in front of him. "I wouldn't have bothered you at all, but I saw your sign out front, and I figure you'll be swamped. I'd like to offer a hand. I'm not as quick as I used to be, but if there's one thing I know how to cook, it's breakfast."

"Oh, Earl, thank you. That would be great."

He stood and rubbed his hands together. "Want me to start with the grits?"

"That's perfect." Despite Earl teaching her how to make grits, hers never tasted quite as good as when Earl made them. Though she didn't care for them either way, she could tell the difference. "Thank you."

He tipped his hat, then hung it on a hook by the door and headed for the kitchen.

Gia started all the coffeemakers brewing.

Savannah carried a hot breakfast pie and put it into one of the glass display dishes. "Are you about ready to open?"

"I think so. There's already a crowd outside." Her stomach fluttered, and she hoped she hadn't gotten in over her head. As much as she wanted to help, she was only one person and could only cook so fast. Even with Earl's help in the kitchen, Willow would be on her own out front. "What time do you have to go to work?"

"I already called out. I'm yours for the day."

"Thanks, Savannah."

"You're welcome."

Gia surveyed the room one last time. Everything seemed to be in order, though Willow wasn't back yet. "As long as you're staying, I think I'll open early and get started. There's quite a crowd building up out there."

"Go for it." Savannah grabbed an order pad and a pen. "I'll take over for Willow for a while."

Gia unlocked the doors. She started seating customers while Savannah took orders and filled coffee mugs.

Cole Barrister walked in, took Gia's hand in his, and kissed her cheek as if they were old friends. "Hello, dear."

"Good morning, Cole. It's good to see you. Would you like a table, or is a seat at the counter okay?"

"Oh, I didn't come in for breakfast. I came to let you know the council meeting has been postponed in light of the tornadoes. It's been rescheduled until Thursday night. I hope you can still make it."

"Oh, definitely. I'll be there." She wouldn't miss it. Between the fire and Willow's story of what happened to her mother, the issue of fire exits needed to be addressed.

"Thank you. Now, where do I find an apron?"

"An apron?" Gia's mind had wandered, and she'd lost track of what he was saying.

"I saw your sign out front. That's very kind of you, but we'd better get started if we're going to serve everyone."

"We?"

"Yes, ma'am. I don't know if I'm ready to take on anything permanently, but I do know I'm ready to help out right now while my neighbors need me."

Gia laid a hand on his arm. "Thank you, Cole."

"No problem. Let's get started. People are looking mighty hungry."

Gia left Savannah to deal with the dining room and headed for the kitchen. After they'd washed their hands and pulled on gloves, Cole jumped right in. Truth be told, he could bang the orders out just as quickly as Gia, probably even quicker once he was back in practice and more familiar with the kitchen setup.

Earl proved to be a big help. He had a knack for seeing what needed to be done and making sure it did.

By midmorning, the three of them had developed a system that allowed them to fill the orders in record time, three times as many as Gia could have done on her own, plus make two rounds of sandwiches to send to the shelter. She sighed. If only this arrangement could be permanent.

Gia put an order up and rang the bell. The older gentleman she kept seeing sat at the same small table in the back corner where she'd first seen him. Only this time, she had the help she needed to go check him out. "Will you two be okay for a few minutes?"

"Yes, ma'am." Cole flipped three eggs smoothly with the long metal spatula without losing a single yolk. "Don't you worry. We're fine."

Earl buttered two pieces of rye toast, cut them, then held the plate out to Cole.

Cole took the plate, slid the three eggs onto it, and dropped a few slices of bacon beside the eggs, while Earl filled a small bowl with grits, then took the entire order to the cutout and hit the bell.

Comfortable they'd manage fine without her for a while, Gia washed her hands and stripped off her apron. Only one grease stain on the bottom of her shirt where something must have splashed beneath the apron. Not too bad considering the morning they'd had.

She smiled as she entered the dining room, greeting people as she wandered through the room.

Esmeralda and Estelle stopped her to let her know how much they'd enjoyed their breakfast and share their storm story.

A group of firefighters, their clothes and faces covered in dirt, stopped her to say thank you for breakfast.

She thanked them for their service and wished them well.

Willow's eyes were still a little puffy, but she wore a bright smile as she seated customers and took orders. She'd left the TV playing behind the counter but had lowered the volume.

Several customers stared at the TV, gleaning information from pictures, headlines, and whatever scrolled across the bottom of the screen.

While Gia strolled through the room, trying to appear casual, she kept the older man in her line of sight.

He sipped his coffee, didn't seem to be in any rush to go anywhere, but didn't bother to look at his menu and didn't seem interested in ordering food when Willow stopped to refill his cup.

Gia stopped beside his table and extended a hand, as she'd done with other customers. "Hi. I'm Gia Morelli. It's nice to meet you."

If his deer in the headlights expression was any indication, he hadn't planned on having to introduce himself. He took her hand. "Sean."

Sean McNeil? He seemed about the right age. She hesitated a moment, hoping he'd add a last name. When he didn't, she tried again. "Are you from around here?"

"Originally."

"Well, what brings you back?"

"Actually, I was just on my way out. Got an appointment to keep." He slid his chair back and stood, leaving his now full cup on the table. "Nice meeting you."

She couldn't think of any way to keep him there, so she reluctantly let him go. "Nice meeting you, too. I hope you'll come again."

"I'm sure I will." He kept his gaze straight ahead as he walked out, then held the door open for someone to enter.

Hank Sanford grunted what might have passed for a thank-you as he strode through the door and headed straight for Gia.

Ah, jeez. She'd finally gotten out of the kitchen and now all she wanted to do was run back there and hide. She stopped at a table and introduced herself to an elderly couple, allowing Willow to greet Hank and offer him a seat, hoping he'd just accept, have something to eat, and be on his way, but her luck wasn't that good.

Hank ignored Willow and homed in on Gia. He marched across the café, jaw clenched, hands balled into fists. Hunt hadn't been kidding when he'd said you should see the other guy. Hank's face was a mess of cuts and bruises.

Gia pasted on a smile. The last thing she needed was a confrontation in the middle of the café. "Hello, Hank. How can I help you?"

He puffed up his chest. "I'm lookin' for Maybelle's cell phone."

"I'm sorry. I haven't seen it, but I can check the lost and found."

He stared hard at her. "Well?"

"Well what?"

"Are you gonna check?"

"Oh, right." Gia headed behind the counter and pulled out a basket of odds and ends people had left behind. An umbrella, a baby bottle—which Gia had cleaned before putting in the basket—and several sweatshirts. No phone. She looked up into Hank's eyes. Even though he could clearly see there was no phone in the basket from where he leaned over the counter, she said, "I don't have it, Hank, I'm sorry. What makes you think she lost it here?"

"The last time she remembers having it was the morning she came in here to talk to you." He had the good grace to blush and look away.

"Well, if anyone had found it, they would have either given it to me or put it in here." She shoved the basket back beneath the counter. "If it turns up, I'll be sure to call."

"Do that." He turned and walked out without so much as a thank-you, clutching his left side as he yanked the door open. Apparently the damage Hunt had inflicted wasn't confined to Hank's face.

Chapter 20

Cole took off his apron and tossed it into the hamper, then stretched. "I have to admit, it felt good to get in front of a grill again."

"Thank you both so much." Gia gave each of them a hug. "I couldn't have gotten through today without you."

"Of course you'd have gotten through." Earl winked. "We just made it easier."

"How about a cup of coffee and something to eat before you go?" Gia locked the door, glad to be done for the day but happy with how things had worked out.

"I wouldn't say no to something small. Maybe one of those chocolate muffins." Cole pointed to a glass cake dish filled with muffins and sat at the counter.

Earl sat on his usual stool two seats over from Cole. "I'll take a blueberry."

Gia placed their muffins on dishes and set them in front of them, then grabbed the coffeepot and started to fill their mugs.

Cole spun around on his stool, leaned back, and rested his elbows on the counter. "I can't believe how much the place has changed since back in the day."

"That's right," Earl said around a mouthful of muffin, "I remember you pitching in behind the bar now and then."

Coffee splashed on Gia's hand. "Ouch."

"Are you all right?" Cole spun back around and took her hand.

"It's fine, thanks." She grabbed a paper towel and dried her hand. "You used to work here?"

"Not really, just lent a helping hand now and again like I did for you today."

"Did you know Sean McNeil?"

"Yes. Good man, Sean."

"Yes, he was," Earl agreed. "Shame what happened to him."

Gia set the coffeepot back on its burner and leaned her folded arms on the counter. "What happened to him?"

Cole gestured to Earl, then bit into his muffin.

Earl sipped his coffee. "Floyd Masters happened to him. Never did like that man, or any other member of the Masters clan. Bunch of no-goods if you ask me."

"Yup, even Floyd's sister's brat." Cole snapped his fingers, his face twisted into a mask of concentration.

"Hayes." Earl's eyes twinkled when he looked at Gia. He knew exactly how she felt about Captain Howard Hayes.

Cole pointed at Earl. "Yeah, that's the one. Thinks he's something special now, but he's no better'n he ever was."

As much as Gia would have loved to hear the Masters' family history, especially when it sounded as if there were a scandal of some sort involved, she needed to get them back on track. "So what did the Masters family do to Sean McNeil?"

"Floyd spent two years trying to shut McNeil down. Wanted to section the building off into apartments, like he had a bunch of other houses in town. Made himself a small fortune buying up houses cheap, then putting tenants in them and collecting rent. Never did maintain any of the houses, though." Earl took another sip of coffee. "Then one day, that kid of his came in."

"Followin' right in his father's footsteps, that one was," Cole added.

"Yes, sir. Apple didn't fall far from the tree in that family. Kid came in one day... What was his name?" Earl scratched his head.

"Frederick," Cole supplied.

"Right, Frederick. Twenty-one years old, barely old enough to drink, and he struts in like he owns the place. Drunk as a skunk and dumber than a bag of rocks, carryin' on about how his daddy was going to own the place."

Cole's expression hardened. "Yeah, but still, Sean shouldn't have served him. He knew better."

"No, he shouldn't have. But I know Sean. He avoided conflict like the plague. Said he just wanted him to go, so he served him a shot and a beer and sent him on his way. Just dumb luck the kid stepped in front of a car." Earl shook his head. "Anyway, after the accident, Floyd Masters made Sean's life miserable. He bad-mouthed him all over town, told people he'd murdered Frederick sure as if he'd taken a shotgun to him. Families stopped coming in. Local businessmen stopped coming in. Pretty soon, Sean was left with a bar full of derelicts he couldn't control."

"Went downhill fast from there, but Sean kept his chin up and tried to make a go of it," Cole said. "Until Sara Mills was killed."

"Yup," Earl agreed.

"What did Sara's death have to do with Sean?" Gia couldn't see a connection, and yet, there had to be one, didn't there?

Earl shrugged.

Cole swallowed a bite of muffin before answering. "No one ever knew, but they were good friends. Then she was killed, and Sean closed up one night and never came back."

"Does anyone know what happened to him?"

Earl looked at Cole.

Cole shook his head. "Not that I ever heard. But I haven't thought about that time in a long while. Funny how you move on to other parts of your life, and twenty years go by before you remember to catch up with people."

"Unfortunately, by then, it's often too late." The sadness had returned to Earl's eyes, and she couldn't help but wonder if he was thinking about his wife.

Earl and Cole chatted a while longer about past mutual acquaintances and town history before agreeing to meet up for breakfast the next morning.

When they were done, Gia thanked them again, locked up behind them, and headed for her office. She flopped into the chair behind her desk, exhausted, and opened her laptop. She only had a minute or two before she had to meet Savannah, but she wanted to see if electricity had been restored to Rolling Pines. Even though she'd packed the small overnight bag, she'd prefer to go home to a nice hot bath.

She stretched her arms over her head. If she was going to continue kayaking, which she definitely wanted to, she'd have to start working out or something. She massaged her back while she waited for the community page to load.

Once it loaded, she scrolled through pictures people had posted of the damage to the development. Downed trees, missing roof shingles, one car that had been crushed beneath a falling tree, another that had overturned. All in all, people considered themselves lucky the damage hadn't been much worse. Six posts down, she finally found what she was looking for. Electricity had been restored.

Gia closed the laptop and shoved it into the oversized canvas bag she used as a purse, but left her overnight bag where it was. It couldn't hurt

Chapter 21

Once Hunt and Leo were gone, Savannah and Gia settled on either end of the living room couch, a bucket of popcorn between them, as they had so many times when they'd lived together.

Savannah pulled a throw from the back of the couch and tucked it around her feet. "What do you want to watch?"

Gia nudged Thor over a bit so she could sit up with her feet on the floor between the couch and the coffee table. She opened her laptop. "Whatever you want is fine."

"Something funny, I think." Savannah used the remote to flip through the channels.

"Before you settle on anything, it's time to keep my promise."

"What promise?"

"I promised I'd help you try to find out what happened to your mother."

Savannah slid forward beside Gia, clicked off the TV, and tossed the remote into a basket of magazines on the corner of the coffee table. "How are you going to do that?"

"Well, for starters, I'm going to finish the search I started last night before the storms hit." She typed *"Floyd Masters"* into the search box.

"You think he has something to do with my mother's death?"

"I don't know, but he was involved in whatever was going on back then, so it's a place to start." She scrolled quickly through the social media sites—she could always go back to them later if she wanted to try to find him—to the Boggy Creek Town website, where the town council members were listed. She clicked on Floyd's name. A small bio appeared beside a picture of an older man with a square jaw, gray hair, and a thick mustache. "Have you ever seen him before?"

"I don't know." Savannah perched on the edge of the couch and leaned closer to the screen. "Maybe. But without the mustache. It's hard to tell."

"The bio says he's been a member for the past twenty years. Even give or take a year or so if this site hasn't been updated in a while, I'm guessing he got on the council after his son was killed."

"Seems like it." Savannah paused. "Council members are elected. See if you can find anything from his election campaign."

Gia typed *"Elect Floyd Masters"* into the search engine.

"Wait." Savannah grabbed her hand before she could hit search and pointed to an article already listed. "Look. There's Floyd's name." She ran her finger along the page. "And here, in the same article, my mother's name."

Gia clicked on the article from a local paper with Savannah leaning over her shoulder and read the headline. *Local Woman Found Dead.* She tilted the screen down. "Are you sure you want to read this? I could read it quick and see if there's anything that will help us."

Savannah stared at the computer, lower lip caught between her teeth.

"Please, Savannah. I'll tell you if there's anything important. I promise." The last thing Savannah needed was to read the details of her mother's death.

She studied Gia a moment, then nodded, stood, and lifted their half-empty glasses. "I'll go refill our drinks. Be back in a minute."

Gia skimmed the article. It didn't take long, as there wasn't much information. A couple of paragraphs detailing Sara's murder and how she was found in her home, and a plea to contact the police with any information. Nothing they didn't already know. Only one line near the end caught her attention.

"Well?" Savannah put Gia's sweet tea on a coaster and returned to her seat.

"Most of it is just a recap of what happened." The details of which Savannah didn't need to hear. "But it says here Floyd Masters was questioned and released."

"What do you make of that?"

"I have no idea, and unless you know how to hack a police computer, I don't know how we can find any details on why he was questioned."

"So, now what?" Savannah slid back and laid her head on the back of the couch, staring up at the ceiling.

"Do you think Leo would check into it?"

"You mean without telling Hunt?" She turned her head to pin Gia with a stare.

"Umm…" On the one hand, she didn't want Hunt to keep her from investigating. On the other hand, if she expected honesty from him, she couldn't very well offer anything less in return. Pursuing a relationship with Hunt might prove a little more difficult than she'd expected. "No, it doesn't matter if he tells him, but I can't very well ask Hunt, since he's suspended."

"True." Savannah stood and grabbed her purse from the corner where she'd dropped it on her way in. She dug through for her phone. "I'll give him a call."

"I'm just going to take Thor out." Gia stood and reached over her head, stretching her back and shoulders, which were probably stiff from bending over the computer. Or possibly still from kayaking, but she hated to think she was that out of shape. She exercised. Sometimes. Once, she even went to the gym. "When I come back, we can watch a movie if you want. Come on, Thor."

Thor scrambled to his feet.

Still spooked about finding the snake on her deck, she clipped the leash to Thor's collar and grabbed the canister of bear spray.

If a dog could sulk, Thor certainly was. He enjoyed running free in the fenced section of the yard.

"Sorry, boy, I can't let you run in the dark. Not yet, anyway." *Maybe not ever.* No way she'd take a chance of him running into something that could harm him. Even with the back light on a motion sensor, she couldn't be sure a snake would be big enough to set it off. Besides, the one on her deck had been lying still for a long time. The light would definitely have had time to turn off. "Just humor me for a little while. I'm working on getting used to this whole snake thing. You can run when it's light out."

Thor groaned.

She flipped on the back light; she wouldn't want to take a chance of it turning off before they were done. After a quick scan of the deck, Gia opened the door and took a tentative step out, holding tight to Thor's leash.

Thor vibrated with the need to get off the deck.

"Come on, boy." She studied the fenced area but didn't see anything, then descended the steps, keeping Thor close. "Be quick."

Gia enjoyed the feel of the cool breeze washing over her. It was unusual in central Florida, but apparently the line of storms that had wreaked such havoc had preceded a cold front. She inhaled deeply, enjoying the feel of the cool, drier air, instead of the chest-crushing heat and humidity.

The smell of smoke wafted to her. Not the lingering smoky smell left over from the fire, but the unmistakable odor of cigarette smoke. What had Hunt said? That the investigator had found a small pile of cigarette butts?

Whoever had started the fire had probably been watching the house for some time. "Come on, Thor."

Thor trotted back to the house at her heel.

She shut the door, flipped the lock, and ran into the living room.

Savannah looked up from the computer as Gia entered. "Is something wrong?"

"I smell smoke outside."

She returned to whatever she was doing on the computer. "Probably left over from the fire, and the wind is carrying it toward the house."

"*Cigarette* smoke."

She looked up again. "Are you sure?"

"Positive. Do you know if Maybelle smokes?"

"No. I don't mean 'no, she doesn't smoke,' I mean 'no, I don't know if she smokes.'" Savannah picked up her phone.

"What are you doing?"

"Calling Leo."

"For what?"

"To see what's going on outside."

"Put the phone down, Savannah. Leo has his hands full dealing with the storm damage. He doesn't need to come running all the way out here to check if one of my neighbors is sitting on his deck smoking a cigarette. Besides, Thor didn't even bark."

"Hunt said a cigarette butt started the fire. If someone was standing out there smoking fairly regularly while watching the house, Thor might have just gotten used to it." She stared longingly at the phone for another moment, then set it aside. "You're right, though, Leo does have his hands full. So, what do you want to do? Ignore it?"

"I can't really ignore it. What if whoever it is starts another fire?"

"All right…" Savannah set the computer aside and ran down the hallway. She returned a moment later with the bat Gia had just started keeping beneath her bed. "Come on. And bring Thor."

"Aye, aye, Captain." Gia couldn't help but smile.

As petite as she was, Savannah wielding a baseball bat made for an imposing figure.

Savannah muttered something that sounded suspiciously like "smart ass" and strode toward the front door.

"Wait." Gia grabbed her arm before she could fling the door open. "What if there's something else out there?"

"Like what?"

"Gia, Savannah, hello." Cole excused himself from a gentleman he was speaking to and greeted them each with a warm hug. He gestured toward the full meeting room, then led them across the lobby to keep from blocking the doorway. "Well, what do you think? Quite a turnout, huh? Better than I'd expected. I don't see how they can say no."

Gia was treading on thin ice. She couldn't share the privileged information Tommy had given Savannah, yet she needed to do something. "Have you figured out where the road could go in yet?"

Savannah leaned close and whispered, "Good luck," then disappeared into the crowd. If Cole should step forward with a solution, Savannah didn't need to be seen talking to him.

"I hadn't really thought about it. I figure at the back would make the most sense. There's a development about five or six miles to the east we could cut over to. Then we could exit from there on already existing roads."

"Who owns the land you'd want to run the road through?" Gia willed him to pick up on her train of thought so she wouldn't have to spell it out.

"I don't think anyone does. It's part of the forest."

"Are you allowed to build there?"

"I don't see why not." He shrugged. "I'd think you could run a dirt road at the least."

"But you're not sure?"

He hesitated. "I'm not positive, no."

"Can you look into it quick before the meeting starts?"

"Uh...sure. Let me make a few calls."

"Thanks, Cole. I'd just like to go before them with as much information as possible. Don't want to give them any excuse to deny our petition."

"You got it." He pulled out his cell phone and headed for the door.

Gia moved through the crowd, saying hello to people who were familiar to her from the café. When she spotted Earl, she stopped. "Earl, what are you doing here?"

"You think I'd let you stand up to the council alone? I'm here to lend moral support, to tell them how much the town needs the All-Day Breakfast Café."

Tears welled in her eyes. "Oh, Earl, thank you."

"You bet." He swept his hand out, gesturing around the room. "I have a sneaking suspicion a lot of these folks will be saying the same thing."

"What are you..."

Savannah waved from across the room, her smile brilliant, obviously happy with the turnout she must have engineered.

"She's a good friend," Earl whispered.

"Yes. She certainly is." Now that she paid more attention to the people in attendance, she recognized more than half of them from the café. These people hadn't come out to support the fire exit, though she hoped most of them would; they came out to support her.

Tears spilled over and trickled down her cheeks. She wiped them away. To think, she'd wasted so much time wondering if she'd made the right choice staying in Florida. If there was any lingering doubt, it fled with the show of support from the community. The community who'd accepted her as one of their own and come together to rally behind her when she needed them. Her community.

Trevor approached and took both of her hands, his smile warm. "It's great to see you, Gia."

"You too, Trevor. Thank you so much for coming."

"You bet." He looked around at the crowd and the people still entering the building. "Hard to believe so many people came out on such short notice."

Gia shook her head, overwhelmed at the show of support. "I don't know what to say."

Trevor grinned. "Just say thank you."

She laughed, still having trouble regaining control. "I will, thank you."

He squeezed her hands, then released her and winked. "I'm going to work the room and drum up any extra support I can get."

The young woman—even younger than Gia had realized—who'd spoken to Gia the night of the fire approached, her toddler on her hip as he had been that night. "Hi, Gia. I'm Nancy, and this is my son, John."

"Nice to meet you, Nancy." Gia shook her hand, then said hello to John.

"Listen, I just wanted to say I'm sorry I was snippy the night of the fire." She shook her head, her cheeks red. "There's no excuse for that, it's just... When I woke up and saw the sky lit up with that orange glow, I was terrified. John and I live alone out there, and I was so scared I wouldn't be able to get him out."

"Don't be silly. Of course, I understand. I would have felt the same way."

"Thank you. And thank you for coming out and speaking about the fire road. I think I'll sleep better at night once it goes in." Nancy laughed a little and wiped the tears from her cheeks. "On a brighter note, after you said your dog woke you the night of the fire, I waited for the sun to come up, then took John straight to the shelter and waited outside for them to open. We got a little female Bernese Mountain Dog puppy, just like yours. Debby assured me she'd be great with John and still protect him if the need arose."

"Well, if she's anything like Thor, Debby is a hundred percent right. Good luck with her. And if you ever run into a problem out there, you are always welcome to knock on my door."

"Thank you, again." Nancy gave her a quick hug with one arm, then hugged John closely as she walked away.

Gia strolled through the room, many people greeting her by name, wishing her luck, promising their support. Many more people talking about the storms and the damage done. The fact everyone agreed it was rare to get such bad tornadoes did little to ease Gia's fears, but at least she wasn't alone.

Scott walked up to her. "Gia. It's nice to see you again."

"Well, if it isn't my knight in shining armor."

They both laughed and shook hands.

Scott gestured to the woman beside him. "This is my wife, Meredith."

Gia shook her hand. "Nice to meet you, Meredith. I hope you'll both come in for breakfast one day. My treat."

"Thank you, we'd love to," Meredith said.

They both wished her luck and moved on.

Gia watched them walk away, realizing nothing united a community the way tragedy did. It seemed the need to help others brought out the best in people.

Maybelle walked out of the ladies' room and stopped short when she almost ran into Gia.

Gia tamped down her feelings. Maybelle did sit on the council after all. "Hello, Maybelle."

Maybelle glared hard at her, then turned her nose up and crossed the room to Hank. She whispered something in his ear.

He looked over at Gia, frowned, and slung his arm around Maybelle's shoulder.

Jeez. So much for being civil. What had she done wrong this time? All she'd said was hello.

"That woman better hope we don't get any more storms. With her nose turned up that high, she'd be lucky not to drown." Willow hugged Gia. "Gia, this is my mom, Skyla."

"Hi, Skyla." She extended a hand. "It's a pleasure to meet you."

Skyla shook her hand. "It's nice to meet you too. I've heard so much about you from Willow. Thank you so much for sending the sandwiches; they were delicious and very much appreciated. You're a good role model for my daughter."

"Thank you so much. Willow is a great kid. I don't know what I'd do without her."

They chatted for a few more minutes. Skyla was everything Gia would have expected from Willow's mother. A free spirit. The kind of woman that encouraged her child to be herself despite what anyone else might think.

Savannah interrupted to let her know the meeting was about to start.

"Well then, I'll see you inside." Skyla wished Gia luck and went to find a seat.

"Are you ready?" Savannah rubbed a hand up and down Gia's arm, practically vibrating with nervous energy.

Gia took a deep breath and let it out slowly. "I think so."

"Come on, then, we don't want to miss the beginning of the meeting." Savannah started into the meeting room.

"Savannah, wait." She held her back. "I don't know how I'll ever thank you for this."

She smiled. "You just did."

"I mean it, Savannah. How in the world did you get these people to come?"

"Actually, I didn't have to coax them at all. I simply let it be known the council would decide the fate of the café tonight, that they'd vote to adhere to the residential zoning or allow the exception. From there, it took off on its own. And people came."

"I can't even believe how many people came."

"Boggy Creek is a small town, Gia. We take care of each other. You supported our community in our time of need. Now they're here for you. It's that easy."

"Well, thank you just the same."

"You're welcome, hon. Now, come on, or you're going to be late. And you need to discuss adding fire exits to some of these developments first." She leaned close and pitched her voice low. "Did Cole find anything?"

Gia glanced around the almost empty lobby. "I don't know. I haven't seen him."

Savannah chewed on her lip and looked around for a minute. "Well, we can't wait. They're starting."

Gia slid into the room just as a frail blond woman took her place at the podium, her hand trembling wildly as she adjusted the microphone to accommodate her short stature. "First I'd like to thank all of you for coming. I'm Brenda Cohen. I'll be standing in as the interim council president until we have time for a vote."

A small round of applause followed.

"Now, if I might, I'd like to ask for a moment of silence to honor Marcia Steers, who served as our president for many years."

Everyone bowed their heads.

Gia's heart ached. Marcia had probably died because she'd been trying to help Gia. The guilt sat like a rock in her gut.

Brenda lifted her head and held her hands up for everyone to remain quiet. "I'd also like to take a moment of silence to honor those of our residents who tragically lost their lives in the devastating storms that affected our area."

Again, everyone remained silent, heads bowed in honor of the dead.

This time, when Brenda stepped back to the podium, a low hum started through the crowd.

She held up her hands, which had steadied a bit, for quiet. "We wanted to postpone tonight's meeting, in light of the recent tragedy, but many of our citizens requested we allow the meeting to go ahead. Would our first speaker please step forward?"

Gia pushed through the crowd at the back of the room and down the aisle to the podium. By the time she reached the front and Brenda had ceded the microphone, the hum had reached an incredible volume. Seemed many residents of Boggy Creek were unhappy with the current fire escape situations.

Gia unfolded a sheet of printer paper she'd jotted her notes on and adjusted the microphone. She cleared her throat, hoping everyone would quiet down without her having to ask. Her insides quivered. She'd never been much of a public speaker, but when Cole had asked her to begin the discussion, she hadn't had the heart to say no. She nodded toward the council members seated at a long table in the front of the room. "Thank you, council members, for allowing me the opportunity to speak on behalf of my community."

The room finally fell silent.

"And thank all of you for coming." She paused and concentrated on the message she wanted to get across before continuing. "I'd like to address a problem that plagues many of our residents, the lack of fire exits at the back of developments."

Chaos exploded: people talking over one another, yelling, demanding action.

Gia waited them out.

Once they realized she wouldn't continue until they settled, they began to quiet down.

"I'd like to ask the council to vote in favor of allowing a fire escape route to be built in the back of Rolling Pines, as well as several other developments. We had people stranded in the middle of bad storms, unable to reach their homes because trees fell or emergency vehicles or accidents blocked the entrances. That's unsafe."

Applause thundered through the room.

"Last week, we had a fire in Rolling Pines. It was brought under control quickly, thanks to local residents and the quick response of the fire department."

Applause and cheers echoed.

"But the situation could have ended in tragedy. A fire at the front of Rolling Pines could trap many of our residents in their homes. We have approximately nine hundred families living in our neighborhood at the base of the Ocala National Forest, where fires are a common enough hazard, and no effective evacuation route."

Maybelle stood and glared at Gia, not even bothering to mask her hatred. "What about the dirt road the park rangers use? Leads up into the forest out the back of Rolling Pines?"

Gia started shaking her head before Maybelle had even finished speaking. Thankfully, Cole had prepared her for that argument ahead of time. "First of all, it leads through miles and miles of forest, and oftentimes it's not passable due to flooding, downed trees, overgrown brush. We need a safe, well-maintained, clearly marked evacuation route."

She searched the crowd for Cole, knowing full well what was coming next and having no counterargument.

Maybelle sneered. "Well, perhaps you should have done your research before wasting everyone's time."

She finally spotted Cole near the front of the crowd. He held his cell phone up discreetly and shook it back and forth.

Maybelle pressed her hands against the table and leaned forward. "You dragged everyone down here at a time when our community is still dealing with one tragedy, when there's no way to build an access road out the back of Rolling Pines even if we wanted to. That's all protected land back there."

"Actually…" Cole stepped forward and Gia shot him a look of gratitude. "There is one section of land toward the back corner on the east side that isn't protected land. It's owned by the town, and as such, the town council has full say on how it's used. So, at this time, we are petitioning the council to use that land as an evacuation route."

Murmurs spread through the crowd.

Maybelle's face paled and she turned to the other council members.

Floyd Masters stood. "Unfortunately, we won't be able to decide on that now. We'd have to look into it further before putting it to a vote."

Savannah's brother, Tommy, stood and addressed Cole. "Would you mind dropping off a map marked with the proposed route you'd like us to consider?"

"Not at all. Thank you."

"Thank you." Gia nodded to Tommy and refrained from shooting Maybelle or Floyd any dirty looks, though it wasn't easy, then returned to stand beside Cole in the back.

Brenda resumed her spot at the podium. "The next order of business is a discussion of the zoning laws regarding the building and property located at 1012 Main Street."

Chapter 24

After hearing person after person speak in favor of keeping the café open, starting with Savannah, Gia declined to make a statement. She figured everyone knew she wanted to keep it open, and there was no sense irritating Maybelle again.

The council members were finally ready to vote.

Brenda glanced repeatedly at Gia, wringing her hands, shuffling through papers, anything to avoid making direct eye contact.

Gia could only assume she wouldn't get her vote. The way she figured it, Brenda, Maybelle, and Floyd would vote against changing the zoning for sure. Tommy would vote in her favor, as would a couple of the other council members Tommy was friendly with. The rest, she had no clue what they'd do.

Brenda approached the podium. "All those in favor of changing the existing zoning to allow the All-Day Breakfast Café to remain open?"

"Aye." All the council members seated at the table raised their hands, including Floyd.

Maybelle glared daggers at Gia, then shot Floyd a dirty look, but she still held her hand up.

Brenda scanned the room. Her gaze caught somewhere in the back corner and held for a moment, then darted away, and she lifted her hand as well.

Cheers went up.

Cole slapped Gia on the back. "Congratulations. You did it."

"Thanks to all of you." Tears spilled over. She couldn't help it. The stress of the past couple weeks had weighed heavily, and now that weight had been lifted thanks to all the people who'd come out to support her.

Earl and Willow made their way through the crowd to offer their congratulations as well.

As happy as she was, Gia couldn't help but wonder what had made everyone vote in her favor and what had caught Brenda's attention before she'd voted.

She searched the crowd for Savannah, hoping she'd have an explanation for the sudden influx of support, and spotted an older man toward the back of the room she was almost positive was Sean McNeil.

Brenda looked around before skulking through a doorway at the front of the meeting room and disappearing into a dimly lit hallway.

McNeil, if it was him, followed a moment later.

Gia caught Savannah's attention near the front of the room and gestured toward the doorway.

Savannah frowned but followed her silent directions.

Gia went after them, accepting good wishes, thanking people, and offering coffee on the house for everyone the next day.

When she finally reached the corridor Savannah had entered, Savannah had already disappeared. Gia followed the corridor, stopping at each intersection and looking down the other hallways before moving on.

She finally spotted Savannah at the end of a long hallway, bent over, her ear pressed against a closed office door.

"Savannah?" Gia called softly, not wanting to startle Savannah, yet not wanting to alert anyone to her presence either.

Savannah pressed a finger to her lips and gestured Gia forward.

Gia crept as quietly as she could, careful to keep her heels from striking the floor. When she finally reached the door, she leaned her ear against it beside Savannah.

An angry man's voice came through the door loud and clear. "I don't care. You were supposed to vote to shut it down."

"What difference would it have made? Everyone else voted to keep it open." The woman she assumed was Brenda spoke quietly.

Gia had to press one ear against the door, cover the other with her hand, and hold her breath to hear her.

"He knew." McNeil's voice raised even louder.

"Who knew what?" Brenda said, her voice trembling.

"Masters. He knew it was me trying to shut it down and buy it. Why else would he have voted in favor of keeping something open he's been trying to shut down for the better part of twenty-two years?" Something crashed. "He had the support he needed to win the vote. He made all his supporters vote in favor of rezoning. It's the only thing that makes sense."

"So you killed Marcia for nothing." Brenda sobbed softly.

"No, I killed Marcia because she was flip-flopping, and I got you on the board in her place. And what did you do?"

He'd killed Marcia. He admitted it. So the whole story about Floyd killing Sara was probably a lie. "Do you have your phone?" Gia whispered.

Savannah shook her head.

"I didn't flip-flop. I had no choice," Brenda cried.

"Of course you had a choice." McNeil's anger was escalating.

Gia had to do something.

"What difference would it have made?" Brenda asked.

"None. I would have lost everything anyway, but at least I'd have known you were loyal. Now, I have no use for you."

"No. Stop. What are you doing?"

Gia stood. She had to get help.

Savannah kept her ear pressed against the door and held up one finger for Gia to wait.

The door ripped open, and Savannah stumbled into the doorway.

A red-faced Sean McNeil grabbed her and shoved her into the room.

Gia started toward them.

Savannah smacked her head on the corner of a desk and crumpled to the floor.

Gia whirled and ran. "Help! Help me!"

McNeil's footsteps pounded behind her, his ragged breathing growing closer and closer.

Gia almost fell as she skidded around a corner without slowing down. Still, McNeil stayed on her heels.

As long as he was following her, Savannah was probably safe. She chanced a quick glance over her shoulder and screamed. "Help!"

"Shut up." He was narrowing the gap between them, and Gia still hadn't reached the meeting room.

She was too winded to yell again without stopping and gasping for breath. He was almost on her.

She rounded another corner, but she was lost. No clue how far away the meeting room was or in what direction. She poured on more speed, turned another corner, and almost plowed right into Cole.

He shoved her against the opposite wall.

She hit the wall, bounced off, and went down hard on her hip.

McNeil barreled around the corner, and Cole plowed his fist into the other man's jaw.

McNeil dropped like a rock.

"Are you all right?" Cole rushed to her.

Gia sobbed and held her hip, unable to get up.

"I'm sorry. I didn't mean to hurt you."

She shook her head. "Savannah," she managed to say.

"Where is she?"

Gia pointed down the hallway she'd come from and struggled to stand.

Thankfully, Cole didn't argue. He simply scooped her up and put her on her feet, then helped her hobble back down the hallway. "I need the police and an ambulance at the town hall."

Confused, Gia looked at him.

He held his phone to his ear with his free hand while trying to explain why he'd knocked someone out without really knowing why.

She glanced back at McNeil.

The man was down for the count, but she still didn't want him to get away.

"Stay." She pointed and hoped Cole understood. "He killed Marcia Steers."

"I'm not leaving you alone."

Footsteps pounded down the hallway, saving her from having to decide.

Leo rounded the corner at a dead run. "What happened? Where's Savannah? Are you all right?"

Gia pointed down the hallway and started walking with Cole for support. "She's down there. She's hurt. McNeil killed Marcia Steers."

Hunt followed a little behind Leo. "Are you all right?"

Gia nodded and a sob escaped.

"I've got this. Go." Hunt stopped and checked McNeil's pulse, then pulled out his cell phone and made a call.

Gia led Leo in the direction she thought she'd left Savannah. It was a pretty direct route back to the office. Somehow while running for her life with a monster on her heels it had seemed more confusing.

Savannah still lay on the floor, eyes closed.

Brenda bent over her, crying softly and begging her to wake up. She looked up when Leo, Gia, and Cole walked in.

Leo fell to his knees at Savannah's side. "Savannah. Wake up."

Cole helped Gia to kneel on Savannah's other side, then guided Brenda away from Leo so he could tend to Savannah. He led Brenda to a chair and placed his hand on her shoulder. Brenda wouldn't be going anywhere.

Gia held Savannah's ice-cold hand and tried to rub some warmth back into her.

"Savannah. Please. Wake up now, honey." Leo smoothed her hair out of her face.

Savannah groaned. Her eyes fluttered and she jerked awake.

"Shh… It's all right, honey. You're okay. Relax."

Gia continued to rub her hand.

"Leo?" Savannah whispered.

"Yes. It's me. Are you all right?"

She frowned and rubbed the top of her head where it had smacked the desk. "I think so."

"Let me see." Leo parted her hair and checked her head. "You've got a nice knot."

"Oh, my—" She tried to get her feet under her.

"Oh, no you don't. You stay right there until the ambulance gets here."

"But Sean McNeil—"

"It's fine. Gia told us, and Hunt already has him in custody."

"But—"

"Look at me." Leo cradled Savannah's cheek and stared into her eyes. "We can sort it all out later. Right now we have just cause to hold him for hurting you and trying to hurt Gia. He's not going anywhere, Savannah, now please relax."

She started to nod, then stopped and held her head in her hands.

"The EMTs will be here in a minute." Leo continued to smooth her hair, his hand trembling.

"Don't make me go in an ambulance," she pleaded.

"Don't worry. I'll be right with you the whole time."

"Thank you."

Leo kissed her hand. "There is one thing you need to know."

"What?" Savannah probed the tender spot on her head.

"I'm not waiting any longer."

Savannah looked up into his eyes. Her lips quivered for a moment before she quickly averted her gaze. "I understand."

"No. I don't think you do." He held her chin and brought her gaze back to his. "I love you with all of my heart, Savannah. I have since we were kids. I've waited for you for most of my life. I can't wait for you any longer. When I knew you were hurt, I couldn't get to you fast enough. When I came through that doorway and saw you lying on the floor, my heart stopped. Please, Savannah, I can't take the thought of being without you.

"I have to be honest, I'd imagined this under much different circumstances this time around, but here goes. Again." He reached into his pocket and took out a small velvet pouch, then opened it and shook a ring out into his hand. "Savannah Mills, will you marry me?"

She threw her arms around his neck and sobbed. "Yes."

Chapter 25

Gia strode through the café, making sure everything was ready before they opened. She expected a good crowd again today, after she'd offered everyone free coffee as a thank-you for their support at the meeting. She checked the row of coffeepots behind the counter, all brewing nicely, the aroma filling the café. Confident she was ready, she unlocked the door and held it open for Earl and Cole. "Good morning, gentlemen."

"Good morning." Earl kissed her cheek.

Cole hugged her. "Good morning."

"Thank you again, Cole. You saved my life."

"Nah. I'm just glad I came along when I did."

"Me too." Gia hugged him once more, then led them to a table near the counter. She and Earl usually shared a cup of coffee at the counter, but a table would be more comfortable for the three of them. She set out three mugs and a stack of plates, added a platter of muffins, then grabbed a coffeepot and placed it on a trivet in the center of the table. "I'm glad you came, Cole. You are welcome to join us anytime you'd like."

"Why, thank you. I'll be sure to come in on my days off."

"Days off? You found a job?" Gia couldn't deny a small sense of disappointment. She'd been hoping he'd accept her offer. Working with him and Earl had been fun.

Cole rubbed his fist, then opened and closed his fingers. "I have to say, hanging out with you sure has proved interesting." He laughed. "Gets the juices flowing, for sure."

She couldn't help but laugh. She liked him too much to be mad at him. She was just glad he'd found something that would make him happy. She filled their mugs. "So, where are you going to work?"

"Right here, I hope. I'll be here bright and early Saturday morning." He held up a finger. "Weekends only, mind you. For now, at least. Maybe one day during the week if you promise to keep things interesting."

She laughed, thrilled that he'd agreed to cook for her. "I promise I'll do my best."

"And I was thinking," Earl said. "I wouldn't mind pitching in now and then too. I enjoyed working with you the other day."

"Oh, Earl, that would be fantastic."

"I can't move like the two of you, but I can do some of your prep work and tend the grill when you're not too swamped. I know it's not much, but it'll give you the opportunity to get out in the front and get to know your neighbors a bit."

"I'd love that, Earl. Thank you so much."

He patted her hand. "Now, what kind of muffins do you have this morning?"

"I tried something new today. Apple cinnamon."

"That sounds delicious." Cole held out his plate. "I'll try one of those, please."

"Me too." Earl held out his plate as well.

Gia served each of them a muffin, then waited to see how they liked them.

"These might be my new favorite," Earl said, after he swallowed his first bite. "It's a toss-up between these and the banana chocolate chip."

"Oh, right. The banana chocolate chip are amazing." Cole took another bite.

Keys rattled in the lock as Savannah unlocked the door and strode through with Leo. "Good morning, all."

Gia jumped up and ran to her. "How are you feeling?"

"I'm fine." Savannah hugged her. "Thank you for hanging around the hospital until they released me. I know you had to get up early."

"Of course. I'd never leave you hurt."

"I know you wouldn't. You're the best." Savannah smiled. She held up her hand, wiggled her fingers, and squealed. Her ring sparkled in the reflection of the overhead lights.

"It's beautiful. I'm so happy for the both of you."

"Me too." Savannah held Leo's arm in both hands and looked up at him. He leaned down and kissed her.

Gia hugged Leo and said hello, then grabbed two more mugs while they sat and Earl and Cole congratulated them.

"Better make that three." Leo pointed to the door where Hunt was about to knock.

Gia unlocked the door and opened it for Hunt.

He leaned down and kissed her. "Good morning, beautiful."

Her cheeks heated. "Good morning."

"I brought you a gift." He held out a shopping bag. "I'll run by and install it as soon as I'm done with breakfast."

Gia opened the bag, peeked inside, and laughed.

"Sorry, babe. I'm getting sick and tired of banging on your door and you not answering. Next time I get stuck out in a tornado, you'll answer right away."

"Bite your tongue, mister. I thought you wanted me to stay in Florida?" Of course, Detective Tall, Dark, and Thoughtful was definitely a plus in the stay column, maybe even enough to make up for an occasional tornado.

Willow knocked on the door, and Gia glanced at the clock and went to let her in. "Hi, Willow. You're early this morning."

"Yeah. I figured with everything that went on last night, you'd be tired, so I came in early to see if you needed a hand."

"Thank you so much." Gia hugged her. "Just a sec. I have something for you."

"For me?"

"Yup." Gia opened the register and pulled out the key she'd had made for Willow. Even though trusting people was hard for her, she was going to have to try. Willow had become a good friend. It was time to start opening up and letting people in. She held the key out to Willow. "Here you go."

"You're giving me a key?"

"It's foolish for you to have to wait for me to lock and unlock the door all the time, and you've proven time and time again how dependable you are, so yes, I'm giving you the key."

"Thanks, Gia. Having the key is special, but not as special as knowing you trust me with it." Willow hugged her, then slid the key onto her Batman keychain and dropped it into her backpack. She waved to everyone at the table. "Good morning, guys. I see you have a full house this morning, Gia."

"Yup. What better way to start the morning?"

"Very true."

Gia grabbed another mug. "Come on in and sit. I have exciting news. Cole and Earl are going to be joining our staff."

"Awesome. Welcome aboard." Willow pulled a chair over from another table and sat.

"Wow, this certainly is the morning for exciting news," Savannah said. "Leo and I got engaged, Cole and Earl got jobs, Willow got a key, Gia got a doorbell…"

They all laughed.

"And Hunt got reinstated."

"Are you serious?" Gia ran over and hugged him.

"Yes. Not only as a detective, but as acting captain pending the investigation into Hayes's involvement in Sara Mills's murder."

"How did you manage that?" Gia replaced the empty coffeepot in the center of the table with a fresh one, then sat down next to Hunt and grabbed a muffin. She'd already tried the apple cinnamon, so she chose a banana nut.

"When Hayes suspended me, and then Leo found his name on the list of people who'd signed out the information on the café, I took everything to Internal Affairs. Questions arose about his involvement. After they looked everything over, they got back in touch. Since I already knew the case and had a history with Hayes, they asked me to help them out, so I was working with them for a while."

"You did seem to know an awful lot of what was going on for someone who'd been suspended." Come to think of it, he'd always said "we" when he was referring to information he'd found.

"That's why I couldn't tell anyone where I was when I went to investigate the Sean McNeil cases. Hayes didn't know at first. I'm sorry I worried you guys."

Gia leaned against his arm. "That's okay. I understand. I'm sure it won't be the last thing you're not able to share with me. And I can live with that, as long as you're always honest."

He kissed her. "That's one thing you'll never have to worry about."

"So," Earl broke in. "What ended up happening?"

"Well. Aside from Hayes being suspended, McNeil was arrested for Marcia's murder, and when we searched his hotel room, we found the missing zoning documents. The search of the surveillance video from the records department showed him entering the building several times a few weeks before Marcia's death." Hunt swiped a hand over his mouth and pushed his half-eaten muffin aside, then clasped his hands on the table. "We were also able to match a ring he wore to an imprint the medical examiner found on the side of Marcia's head, so we have a strong case against him."

"That, and Brenda turned on him before they even got her into an interrogation room," Leo added.

"That's a real shame," Cole said. "The Sean McNeil I remember was a nice guy."

"Years of torment at the hands of Floyd Masters seem to have taken their toll," Hunt said. "He wanted his life back, and I guess Marcia stood in the way of that."

All of them sat quietly for a few minutes. Then Earl asked, "What about Masters? Seems unfair for him to walk away unscathed after causing so much trouble."

"Don't worry, Masters isn't walking away." Hunt looked right at Savannah. "There's no statute of limitations on murder. The Sara Mills case has been reopened. It's too early to tell if we'll be able to get him for the murder, but we're hopeful. I'm expecting the DA to offer McNeil a deal if he'll testify, but we'll still have to find evidence. The list Hayes buried at the time is a good start."

Tears shimmered in Savannah's eyes, then tipped over her lashes and ran down her cheeks. She made no move to wipe them away. "Thank you, Hunt."

"You're very welcome, little cousin."

Gia sat back and blew out a breath.

"What about Maybelle?" Savannah wiped her cheeks. "Did you find out how her phone ended up at Gia's?"

Hunt shook his head. "Best we can figure, she must have dropped it while looking for Hank. We did find out how she knew you two were at Marcia's house with Leo and me the day Marcia was killed, though."

"How?" That had bothered Gia a lot, because she'd worried someone Hunt or Leo had trusted with the information had betrayed them.

"One of Marcia's neighbors identified Maybelle's car, said she used to see her sitting outside of Marcia's late at night when she went to walk her dog before bed. She took the license plate number one day, in case anyone got robbed. Her car was there several times throughout the day Marcia was killed."

"Apparently, she had a clue what Hank was doing long before anyone realized," Gia said.

"Yup. Anyway, I gotta run. I have to be at the station for a meeting with the DA in about an hour." Hunt pushed his chair back and stood, then lifted the bag he'd given Gia. "And this doorbell isn't going to install itself."

Gia walked him to the door. "Will I see you later?"

"You bet. I was thinking leftover barbeque tonight, sound good?"

"Mmm...yummy."

He brushed his lips against hers. "Then maybe a movie?"

"Something funny?"

"Perfect." He kissed her once more, then opened the door.

Gia watched him go, then turned back to the rest of her family. Content in a way she hadn't been for a very long time, Gia flipped the sign to open. It felt good to finally know she was home.

If you enjoyed *Murder Made to Order*, be sure not to miss the first book in Lena Gregory's All-Day Breakfast Café Mystery series!

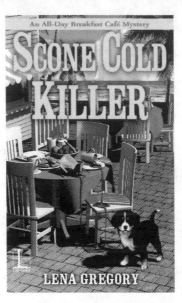

For Florida diner owner Gia Morelli, there's no such thing as too much breakfast—unless it kills you….

When Gia Morelli's marriage falls apart, she knows it's time to get out of New York. Her husband was a scam artist who swindled half the millionaires in town, and she doesn't want to be there when they decide to take revenge. On the spur of the moment, she follows her best friend to a small town in central Florida, where she braves snakes, bears, and giant spiders to open a cheery little diner called the All-Day Breakfast Café. Owning a restaurant has been her lifelong dream, but it turns into a nightmare the morning she opens her dumpster and finds her ex-husband crammed inside. As the suspect du jour, Gia will have to scramble fast to prove her innocence before a killer orders another cup of murder….

A Lyrical Underground e-book on sale now.
Keep reading for a special look!

"Yup. I had my brother, Joey, extend the closet to the back wall, so you didn't even lose that much storage space. I figured you'd want your office to be right by the door, though, so you can still hear what's going on in the kitchen and the café if you leave the door open."

"It's amazing, thank you." She threw her arms around her friend's neck. "You've done so much for me, Savannah."

"That's what friends are for." Savannah hugged her, then stepped back. "I'm just glad you're out of there now. I was worried sick every time you went back."

"I know. I'm sorry."

"Don't be silly. It wasn't your fault." She lowered her gaze, but Gia didn't miss the flash of anger in her eyes. "I'm just glad you're here and ready to start over."

Gia just nodded. There was really nothing to say. Her divorce had been a bitter disaster, played out in the media for the whole world to see. Everywhere she'd gone, she'd been hounded by reporters—when she was lucky. On the worst days, her husband's victims had been pounding on her door and blowing up her phone.

The only respite she'd had through the entire ordeal had been the weekend escapes during which she'd managed to set up her shop. Thankfully, she'd been smart enough to keep working throughout her marriage, despite Bradley's insistence that she quit. Between that nest egg and the meager divorce settlement that was left after the lawyers and victims had been compensated, she'd been left with just enough to put a down payment on the beautiful building that housed the café and upstairs apartment and to buy a small house. She'd thought about living in the apartment for a while, and had stayed there on her brief visits, but she really wanted a place to go home to separate from the cafe. Of course, she wished she'd seen the house first, but beggars can't be choosers, and it was pretty much all she could afford anyway.

A loud crash from outside the back door startled her. She jumped and whirled toward the sound. A tremor shook her. Sweat sprang out on her forehead and trickled down the side of her face.

Something squeezed her shoulder.

Gia practically jumped out of her skin.

Savannah jerked her hand back and frowned. "Are you all right?"

How could she explain the panic attacks she'd suffered this past year? How could she reveal the paranoia, the prickling sensation at the back of her neck that would come over her at random moments, the absolute conviction that someone was watching her? How could she tell Savannah about the death threats she'd received without making her worry even more? Easy, she couldn't. "I'm sorry. I'm fine. You just startled me." She forced a laugh. "What was that noise, anyway?"

Savannah's eyes narrowed, and she stared at Gia for a moment longer, then, thankfully, she let the matter drop. "Sounded like the dumpster in the parking lot out back."

Desperate to escape the claustrophobia threatening to suffocate her, as well as Savannah's far too observant gaze, Gia shoved open the back door.

The instant she emerged from the air-conditioned shop, the humidity slammed into her chest. Her breath shot from her lungs as if she'd gotten punched.

Savannah's laughter helped shake the last of the paranoia that had gripped her. "Don't worry. You'll get used to it."

"I'm not so sure."

"Trust me. It won't take long before you're looking for a jacket when the temperature falls below seventy."

"Somehow, I doubt—" She stopped short, not sure what exactly she was looking at. A man, clad in dirty, threadbare jeans, hung from the dumpster.

"Harley? Is that you, Harley?" Savannah strode toward the dumpster, then stopped and propped her hands on her hips. "You get down from there right now. What has Trevor told you about taking stuff out of dumpsters?"

The man pulled his upper body out and swung himself down to the concrete. His cheeks flushed, though whether from the intense heat or embarrassment, Gia had no clue. He lowered his gaze to the ground and smoothed a hand over his scruffy, more-gray-than-blond beard. "Sorry, ma'am."

Savannah's tone softened. "Don't be sorry. You didn't do anything wrong, but you're going to get sick if you eat stuff out of dumpsters." She reached as if to put a hand on his arm.

He lurched back.

"It's okay, Harley. But if you're hungry, just ask. You know that."

He nodded, glanced longingly at the dumpster once more, then headed off across the parking lot, slowed by a bad limp.

"Harley?" Gia called after him.

He stopped and turned but didn't make eye contact.

"I'm opening tomorrow, and if you come in, I'll treat you to breakfast on the house."

He nodded and started away again.

Savannah leaned close, pitching her voice low. "He won't come inside."

She didn't know his story, but something about him touched her. Perhaps the lost look hovering just below the surface in his bright blue eyes. She yelled after him. "I'll leave a bag out back, right beside the door."

He waved over his shoulder but kept walking.

Gia stared after him, as he shuffled across the remainder of the parking lot, his gait steady but stilted, and disappeared into a bunch of trees bordering the lakefront park. "What's up with him?"

"Don't worry about Harley. He's harmless. Everyone around here..." She gestured toward the row of shops behind them. "Well, they sort of take care of him."

"He's homeless?"

Savannah shook her head. "I don't really know, but he won't even go inside a building, so I assume so."

"Where does he live?"

"Wherever he can find somewhere to hang out."

"What about when it rains?" Weird how she'd walked past dozens of homeless people every day back home, without ever really seeing them as individuals, but this one man touched her in a way they hadn't. She wished she could go back and take notice, see each of them as a unique person with their own story, their own tragedy.

"The park has picnic areas and other sheltered spaces without walls. Technically, he's not allowed to be there, but no one chases him away. Now, come on."

"Huh? Come on where?" She shook off her concern. She'd leave something for him to eat when she closed tomorrow. Hopefully, he'd take it. "Where are we going?"

"To see your new house, silly. I'm so happy you got here in daylight."

A small thrill coursed through her. Her very own house.

"And I assume you'll want to come back to the café afterward..."

Gia nodded as she held the door for Savannah to reenter the shop, then hurried through after her. "I want to make sure everything is perfect for tomorrow. I'll probably do a lot of the prep tonight."

"So we should swing by the shelter on the way to the house."

"Shelter?" The glass-domed cake dishes lining the counter distracted her from whatever Savannah was going on about. They'd be perfect to display quiche and breakfast pies, a variety of muffins, and scones. A row of stools allowed for counter seating, which would give her room for an extra ten or twelve customers. She started counting the stools.

"Yeah. Can you believe they just shut down a pet store last week? The animal shelter is overloaded with puppies."

Her concentration faltered, and she lost count. "Puppies?"

"Yeah." Savannah grinned.

"You're getting a puppy?"

"No, you are."

"Why in the world would I do that?" The thought of a pet was appealing. She'd never had one before, not even as a kid, and the company would be nice, but she'd probably choose something less... intense. Like a fish, or maybe a parakeet.

"For protection."

Hmm... She hadn't thought of that. Her ex had left some very angry former clients in his wake, some of whom had pounded on her apartment door and others who had gone into the deli where she worked looking for her on more than one occasion. But surely they wouldn't find her over a thousand miles away. And, hopefully, whoever had sent the death threats wouldn't follow through on his promise to hunt her down. Okay... a dog might not be a totally bad idea. "I doubt any of Bradley's..." The name left a sour taste in her mouth. "Victims would follow me to Florida."

"Well, you never know. And you'll be living out at the edge of the forest alone, so you'll get a dog, because it'll make me feel better." She grabbed her bright orange canvas bag from the counter, fished out her car keys, and opened the front door. "Besides, a dog will warn you if there're any bears around."

Wait. What! "Bears?"

"Coming?" she tossed over her shoulder with an innocent smile as she walked out.

"Hey," Gia called, running after her. "You're kidding about the bears, right?"

Meet the Author

Lena Gregory lives in a small town on the south shore of eastern Long Island with her husband and three children. When she was growing up, she spent many lazy afternoons on the beach, in the yard, anywhere she could find to curl up with a good book. She loves reading as much now as she did then, but she now enjoys the added pleasure of creating her own stories. She is also the author of the Bay Island Psychic Mystery series, published by Berkley. Please visit her website at www.lenagregory.com.

Printed in the United States
by Baker & Taylor Publisher Services

Chapter 1

"I'm just surprised you got out of New York without killing that son of a—"

"Savannah!" The harsh sentiment hurled with all of Savanah's sweet, easy-going, southern-girl charm caught Gia Morelli off-guard, and she stared at her best friend.

"What?" Feigning innocence, Savannah propped a long, hot pink nail beneath Gia's chin and shoved her mouth closed. "It's September in Florida, honey. You keep that open too long, you're bound to get a mouthful of lovebugs."

"What's a lov—" Gia waved her off. "Never mind. It doesn't matter."

"All that matters is that you're here now." Savannah hefted Gia's overnight bag from the back seat of the cab she'd taken from the airport while Gia paid the driver. As the cab pulled away, Savannah slung her free arm around Gia's waist. The four inch heels on her sandals only brought her to Gia's chin. "I'm just glad it's over."

If that wasn't the understatement of the year...

Gia wrapped her arm around Savannah's shoulders and squeezed. "Me too."

The two of them stood together on the sidewalk, staring up at the glossy new sign above the shop—Gia's shop—door. *All-Day Breakfast Café*. A Grand Opening banner hung limp in the humidity beneath it.

Gia's gut cramped. The hot Florida sun threatened to melt the makeup right off her face. The long skirt, light sweater, and knee-high leather boots that had left her slightly chilly in the brisk, early-morning, fall air in New York a few hours ago, were practically suffocating her now. She wiped her forehead, ignoring the flutter in her stomach and the fact that her nerves, rather than the stifling heat, were probably making her sweat.

"Enough of that. Come on. Let me show you what I've done with the place since you were here last." Savannah's growing excitement was contagious.

The knot of tension loosened a little.

"I was just making sure everything was ready when the taxi pulled up." She grinned and started forward. "I thought you weren't coming in until tonight?"

Gia shrugged, not yet ready to explain her need to escape sooner. She forced a smile. "Last-minute change of plans."

"Well, I'm glad you're here to stay this time." Savannah weaved her fingers through Gia's and squeezed her hand. "But you should have called me. I'd have picked you up at the airport."

Gia glanced at her, trying to hide the pain and fear she knew her friend would see anyway. "Thanks, Savannah. I know you would have, but I needed to do it myself."

A brief flicker of pity softened Savannah's expression, but then a smile emerged. She tugged on Gia's hand, then released her and started toward the front door. "Well, you're home now. And wait until you see the finishing touches I've made to the shop. You're going to love them."

Gia took another moment to admire the historical, two-story building that housed the shop. *Her* shop. The pale yellow paint with white trim had been a great color choice. Standing proudly on one corner, it fit nicely with the other shops along Main Street in the small, artsy, tourist town of Boggy Creek. Nestled a bit south of Central Florida's Ocala National Forest, the town was known for its festivals, art and craft shows, and seasonal fairs. Her breakfast café would be the perfect addition. She hoped.

Shaking off another attack of nerves, she caught up to Savannah where she'd waited on the walkway.

"I can't believe you're finally here to stay this time," Savannah said.

"Me neither." The past year, since she'd found out about her husband's— *ex*-husband's—illicit and illegal activities, had flown by in a blur of confusion and betrayal. Savannah had been her rock, the one person who'd steadied her and helped her move toward a future. "Flying down for a day or two at a time wasn't easy."

"No, it wasn't, but you did it," Savannah reminded her, then gestured toward the café. "And just look what you've got to show for it."

Pride surged. "You're right."